CW00348470

Tales For Children From The Jurassic Coast

by

Tony Lambert

Tony Lambert

This is a First Edition of the paperback
Tales For Children From The Jurassic Coast

ISBN: 978-1-910094-01-3

eBook ISBN: 978-1-910094-41-9

Published March 2016
By Magic Oxygen
www.MagicOxygen.co.uk
editor@MagicOxygen.co.uk

Editing team: Toni McKee, Ariel Pimentel, Simon West, Tracey West

A catalogue record for this book is available from the British Library.

Printed by Lightning Source UK Ltd; committed to improving environmental performance by driving down emissions and reducing, reusing and recycling waste.

View their eco-policy at www.LightningSource.com

Set in 11.5pt Times New Roman

Titles set in Peleja

Contents

You are about to enjoy Tales For Children From The Jurassic Coast and you might be interested in becoming a Go Jurassic Ranger.

Go Jurassic is the club for young fans of the Jurassic Coast's fossils and dinosaurs, and membership is £30 for 12 months.

Our Rangers receive an ammonite t-shirt, badge, passport, plus regular newsletters and other goodies. We also run a range of fabulous events for our Rangers like fossil hunts, behind-the-scenes tours and museum nights at various locations all along the Jurassic Coast.

Go Jurassic! is run by the Jurassic Coast Trust, the charity which funds and inspires conservation, understanding and community engagement along the 95 miles of World Heritage Coastline.

We fund training sessions for our Ambassadors like Tony, who then use their expertise to engage people of all ages with the incredible stories of the Jurassic Coast.

See JurassicCoast.org for details

This Book is Dedicated to

The Jurassic Coast Trust
for all their support

Boxes of Temptation

Introduction

In January 2007, a large container ship called the Napoli beached on the pebble banks off Branscombe beach on the Jurassic Coast in East Devon.

The decision to run the Napoli aground was made by the crew after she sustained severe storm damage which put the vessel in grave danger of breaking up, sinking its containers and spilling its oil. Many of the containers dislodged and plunged into the sea and a great many of them washed up right on Branscombe beach. For several days afterwards, this usually quiet village had to cope with an onslaught of treasure seekers!

This particular part of the Devon coast could roll out countless tales from its long history of smuggling and contraband and the surprising arrival of boxes packed full of tempting goods quickly aroused a spirit of adventure in some of the younger local inhabitants.

This story recounts the dramatic events as they unfolded and follows the actions of a few souls who used their knowledge of the area to avoid the crowds as they forged subversive plans to profit from the misfortune of the Napoli, but to what end?

In the warm front room of his home situated up a long valley in the Devon seaside village of Branscombe, Johnny Watson sat watching the late evening local news.

His parents and older brother Leo were also watching the shocking images of the gigantic Napoli, a container ship loaded to capacity, struggling to make headway through huge waves and near hurricane force winds in a violent Atlantic storm heading eastwards along the English Channel.

The reporter, protected by a bulky waterproof jacket, held his hat in one hand and a microphone in the other as he tried to shout above the howling wind as the sea spray mercilessly lashed Sidmouth promenade.

"We understand," he yelled into the microphone, "that the vessel, which was en route to South Africa, is now in great difficulty as a result of this extremely bad weather. There are fears that some of its 2,400 containers could be washed overboard tonight and perhaps worse still, the vessel could break up and sink. We also believe there to be 3,500 tonnes of fuel oil on board, which of course raises the possibility that this could cause a colossal environmental disaster all along the south coast."

Following the news bulletin there were family mutterings and comments about climate change, global trade and unsafe vessels ploughing their way across the world's oceans. Johnny decided it was time to go to bed.

The next morning being a Saturday, and with no desperate desire to do his homework, Johnny decided to get up early and join his Mum, Dad and Leo on a walk to the beach café, about a mile away across the fields. As they approached the beach, they noticed there were far more people than usual for a blustery February morning and they all appeared to be heading in the same direction. Once they'd passed the café and stepped onto the beach, they soon realised why.

Right in front of them, in clear view about a mile off Branscombe beach, was the container vessel they'd seen and heard about on the news the night before. Nobody bothered to put the television on before they left the house so the image of this listing hulk stacked with big containers loaded up to four levels high above the deck, was an horrific sight to behold. Johnny's Mum put her hand to her mouth and he could see tears in her eyes as they joined the ever increasing crowd of onlookers staring out to sea. Although the Napoli was beached quite a way offshore, the sheer size of the vessel made it seem ever so much closer.

Eventually, the family walked home cross and anxious, wondering why this vessel and its disastrous cargo of destruction had been allowed to end up at the beach they loved so much, along this beautiful part of the Jurassic Coast.

Further news bulletins were eagerly watched as the drama unfolded and they learned their lovely beach was favoured to settle the stricken vessel because of its massive offshore pebble banks, rather than risking it sinking in deeper water, causing even greater chaos.

The next day, everyone headed to the cliff tops for another look at this unbelievable spectacle. The usually empty fields that led to the cliff edge were filled with vehicles topped by large satellite dishes and countless reels of cables snaked through the grass as on the spot reports were broadcast around the world. Many of the containers had cascaded into the sea and were busily being washed up between Branscombe beach, right across to Beer Head and beyond to Beer and Seaton.

As darkness approached, Leo told his parents he was heading off to see friends in Beer. Just before the pubs closed, Leo, together with his friends Pete and Jay, walked up to the cliff top, then headed back towards Branscombe beach. Being local lads, they knew the well-trodden and some of the not so commonly used paths and tracks down the cliff to the beach.

As their boots scrunched on the pebbles, they looked around carefully to ensure they really were alone; there were no voices and no lights. They scanned the tide line carefully with their torches right down to the slope of the beach. They were close to Beer Head at the eastern end of Branscombe and in the tricky darkness, they traced the shadowy outlines of around 10 large containers, some of which had been smashed against the rocks, scattering their contents far and wide.

There were random items of clothing, some personal belongings, cosmetics and further along the beach there were plastic car parts, large empty wooden barrels and some heavier, smaller barrels full of wine, scattered from the tide line right up to the base of the cliffs.

Leo and his friends stuffed all sorts of interesting small items into their backpacks, then as other torch lights approached them, became suddenly aware that they weren't alone at all! They grabbed their bags and ran for cover behind some big boulders nearby, believing the torch lights to be in the hands of either patrolling policemen or security guards. The lights got closer and closer and the three of them huddled up, tighter and tighter, doing their best to avoid being spotted. The rhythmic sound of footsteps on the pebbles stopped for a moment and Leo poked his head tentatively around the rock. A beam of light caught him full in the face; he gasped, silence followed, then a voice called out from the tide line.

"Who is it?"

"I dunno," came the reply from the man who'd spotted Leo.

"Just some bloke."

The crunching sound of footsteps on pebbles recommenced as the other group continued westwards along the beach, clearly intent on scavenging the battered boxes. Leo and his mates conceded they'd had enough excitement for one night and hastily retraced their steps back to where Leo had left his car.

The next morning, Leo left early for work as usual. Johnny went to meet the school bus and Mum headed off to the school she worked at in nearby Honiton. After listening to Leo's dramatic tale after he arrived home late the previous evening, Dad decided to get his camera and go and explore the beach too. The car park for the beach café was full of media vehicles all poised for action with their powerful satellite dishes, together with a portable office that the police were using. Hordes of people were emerging from footpaths and down the narrow access road to the beach. It seemed the catastrophe had been so widely reported, people from all over the country - and even from other countries - along with many locals, were down on the beach scurrying around to see what they could find.

Reports of brand new, top of the range motor bikes being found in some containers were true, but the numbers were wildly exaggerated. One of the daily newspapers reported Branscombe beach as, 'A treasure trove waiting to be emptied.'

The police attempted to seal off access to the beach from the café car park but Dad, alongside many others, simply walked up the field to the caravan park, then descended to the beach from there. The police soon realised their attempts to restrict access had failed miserably so they stood back and watched as the ever increasing flood of people carrying empty boxes, backpacks and bin bags, walked past them.

Later that day, a couple of police officers started handing out forms to those leaving the beach laden with booty, advising them to fill them in and declare what they'd removed, thereby avoiding possible subsequent prosecution.

Dad was amazed and horrified at the devastation that surrounded him. So many huge metal boxes, some still grouped together in clusters of four, were ripped open, their guts spewed all over the beach. A smashed wooden crate had thoughtlessly strewn the personal belongings of a family all across the pebbles. There were also bags of dog food and nappies too. Empty wooden barrels lined up one after another along the flat ridges and soaking wet rolls of carpet and expensive looking rugs piled up near the water's edge.

A bizarre mix of steering wheels and pots of expensive cosmetics greeted the hungry treasure hunters and they stuffed all and sundry into their boxes and bags. There were engine parts too and a handful of vehicles with zero miles on the clock which had been crushed almost out of recognition within their flimsy metal casings.

Dad took a photo of an upside down, half-buried tractor, one of many during his couple of hours on the beach. The only scavenging he did was rescuing a Pooh-Bear glove puppet, its face and open arms peeping out from under the corner of a heavy barrel.

As day darkened to night, the steady flow of people arriving failed to cease. Fires were lit to keep looters warm and children played amongst the debris long after nightfall, as the relentless actions continued into the wee hours. Some items were initially dragged from the beach only to be abandoned around the village and neighbourhood wheely bins were unceremoniously emptied so that booty could more easily be wheeled back to their cars and vans, some were so pumped full of adrenaline, they couldn't even remember where they had parked and they rambled aimlessly through the darkened streets.

Residents near the access roads experienced a night like no other, as constant traffic made proper sleep virtually impossible. The following day the police introduced a one-way system, a measure which was quickly halted after residents complained strongly at a public meeting in the village hall; it was nothing short of absolute chaos in Branscombe.

During the week that followed, life gradually returned to normal as police controls monitored folks coming in and going out of the village and heavy equipment was brought in to remove the debris and clear up the mess. Teams of beach cleaners collected countless bags of rubbish and gradually Branscombe beach's former beauty was slowly restored.

This operation continued both on land and at sea for several weeks and a long oil slick which started to seep out of the stricken vessel after it was first grounded, spread along the coast as far as the beaches of Dorset, affecting the lives of distressed sea birds caught up in its black gooey mess.

The sea remained mostly calm as the Napoli's remaining cargo of oil was sucked out and pumped into another vessel. A huge barge and a tall crane from Holland started to remove some of the containers and transferred them to a nearby port. All was going well until a bout of low pressure and more bad weather swept in from the Atlantic, halting all operations.

The rough seas returned - thankfully not as bad as before - and a further handful of containers became dislodged and plunged into the ocean waves. Five of them washed up on the western side of Branscombe beach at a place called Littlecombe Shoot.

When Leo heard the news he became quite excited at the thought of another adventure. It was a Friday evening and Leo told his parents he was off to investigate on his own. Johnny wanted to go with him but Leo had no intention of letting his 13 year old brother spoil his fun and anyway, Johnny had badly sprained his ankle during a football match a couple of days before, so he was in no fit state to tackle the steep narrow paths down the cliff.

After tea, Leo set off with his backpack full of what he needed for the rest of the evening. He drove to the church, parked his car and took the public footpath from the graveyard through the woods to the cliff top. Just as before, he took the clearly defined path which zigzagged past a few summer chalets, discretely hidden amongst the trees, all the way down the slope of the cliff and onto the beach.

Down at Littlecombe Shoot, the scene was most depressing. One of the containers had become completely grounded after the last high tide and another was almost squashed flat, having disgorged its cargo of multi-packs of chocolate biscuits across the landscape. The other three were stuck on the rocks. Leo couldn't reach them as the tide wasn't low enough; there was no one to be seen in either direction.

He wandered over to the large green container which was securely padlocked. He walked around it twice and it occurred to him that it might contain something of interest but there was nothing he could do at that point in time. As for the other three, he'd have to wait for the tide to go out further.

He telephone home to check the time for low tide and would have to wait a couple of hours but he had several cans of drink in his bag, he was warm, patient and it wasn't raining. After a while, he stood up and voiced a few loud wishes concerning his ideal choice of contents in the three boxes on the rocks. He was really surprised that after all that had happened, he was still quite alone on the dark beach. Only the distant lights of the Napoli and its two guardian ships moored close by, were to be seen.

After an hour or so, with the help of his head torch, Leo managed to carefully walk across the rocks to reach two of the three stranded containers. They weren't as robust as the one on the beach and he managed to break the seals with his pocket knife. He lifted and levered open sections of the door wide enough to shine his torch inside and took a few photographs with his mobile phone. Inside, the contents were large, oily and quite probably machinery of some sort, so he closed the doors and replaced the seals as best as he could. Once he was back on the beach he examined the other container once more before heading off to the car.

"Well," said Johnny as soon as Leo walked into the front room. "What did you find then?"

Leo showed the family the photos and told them what he'd seen. An hour or so later, Johnny heard his brother on the phone to one of his mates who lived near Beer. Leo was standing outside by the car port chatting to his friend. Johnny sneaked into the toilet by the front door and through the open window, he could just about overhear the conversation. They were making plans to meet up the following evening.

"OK mate," said Leo, "I'll see you at the church at 7.00 o'clock tomorrow night and we'll see what we can do – bye!"

At 6.45pm the next day, Leo left the house wearing warm clothes and boots. During the day they'd seen a few images on the television of the most recent containers washed ashore at Littlecombe Shoot. All entrances to the village continued to be manned by police who were checking everyone coming in and going out.

Johnny told his parents he'd arranged to stay overnight with a friend near the Mason's Arms pub in the village. Dad offered him a lift down but Johnny said he'd rather go on his bike, despite his swollen ankle. He left home with a small rucksack and made his way to the church where he knew Leo would have left his car. Sure enough, there were two cars there; Leo's VW and a small Ford which he supposed belonged to Jack, Leo's friend from Beer. He hid his bike behind the church wall then taking the same path as his brother, he limped his way from the graveyard up through the woods to the cliff top.

Without putting too much pressure on his aching ankle, he made his way slowly down the cliff path. He didn't have a torch but like Leo, he knew the route well and it wasn't too challenging.

The last small chalet just before the beach was called Crab Pot and as Johnny approached it, he heard Leo and Jack whispering on the little patio. He knew he mustn't get caught, as Leo would be furious. Johnny made his way around the back and froze when he heard them walk past. What on earth had they been looking at, he wondered?

He emerged from behind the chalet and crossed over the path to the patio where he had a good view of the beach below, surprisingly good in fact, as a bright security light had been set up to illuminate the stranded boxes. However, although the light was bright it only lit up half the padlocked container. Johnny leant against the rail around the patio, took the weight off his ankle for a while and watched.

Leo and Jack had also noticed that part of the beached container was in shadow and carefully made their way along the dark top ridge of the beach towards the big green box. From underneath his coat, Jack produced two brand new hacksaw blades to deal with the pair of padlocks which tightly secured the bars across the access doors. They both put gloves on, then set about sawing through each padlock to release the bars and hopefully open the door. They felt quite sure that if they kept in shadow all the time, they'd be OK.

After fifteen minutes they'd successfully sawn through one padlock and were well through the second one when Jack paused for a moment to look out to sea. He noticed a small boat, not far off the shoreline with a search light that was scanning the beach. They hadn't noticed it before as they had had their backs to the sea. Maybe it had been there all the time with its light switched off? They stopped what they were doing and went cold with fright as they both clearly heard voices, not coming from the boat, but from the beach.

Dropping their blades in haste, they started to panic and instantly decided that it was time to leave. They ran back along the top ridge, then with increasing panic, saw six torch lights coming towards them. The beams of light were bobbing up and down rapidly and the people in hot pursuit were clearly running at a pace.

Someone shouted, "Get those looters! Stop them before they reach the path!"

Leo stopped running. No way would they make it to the path by the Crab Pot chalet. Just to his left, he spotted a large flat rock partially hidden by the undergrowth. On top of the rock there was a barely visible white mark – Leo's heart leapt. He remembered this spot. He'd seen it before but not for many years; it was a way out, an overgrown escape route to the top of the cliff. The six lights in front of them were getting very close, he grabbed Jack's arm.

"Quick, follow me this way!"

They both jumped into the bushes and disappeared into the undergrowth as Leo's brain desperately tried to remember how to follow the old path which led round the back of Crab Pot to rejoin the main footpath higher up. His memory was good and they beat a hasty retreat to freedom without any light along the tangled path. They tripped over roots and stones and scratched their legs and hands on the way as they raced past large prickly bushes growing along the old hidden path. Further up it, they miraculously avoided sliding down its many exposed and eroded edges with sheer drops of tens of metres down to ever more tangled undergrowth.

Meanwhile, back down on the beach the security guards who had been brought in from other parts of the country shone their torches around furiously as they bashed their way through the spiky bushes in a vain effort to catch the two fugitives. There was much shouting and swearing and by the time they eventually reached the main path, Leo and Jack were long gone, their bloodied legs still racing along the good path to the top of the cliff and down to their waiting cars.

When Johnny heard the shouting and saw the torches, he quickly hid in the bushes next to Crab Pot and waited. He heard the men chasing Leo and Jack and eventually, exhausted by their futile efforts, he watched the guards return down the main path, passing very close to his hiding place, on their way back to the beach.

Johnny stayed hidden for some time. He tried to doze off but his uncomfortable position deep in the bushes made it impossible, so he crawled out and crept over to the chalet patio. He could hear the guards talking just below him. One of them was almost shouting down his mobile phone; clearly the reception wasn't very good.

"How long did you say?" he queried. "Sorry, didn't hear what you said there. Listen, we have two guys here with badly cut legs and they need treatment, maybe even a few stitches."

There was a pause.

"Yes, they can walk - just about."

There was another pause.

"Righto, we'll make our way back to the café but Ed says he'll stay here as he's OK. Tell me again how long will it be before the other guys arrive?"

Another short pause ensued.

"Fine, I'll tell Ed. See you later." He must have turned to his colleague Johnny imagined, then said, "They'll be here in about an hour Ed. That all right with you?"

"Yeah, no probs. You get off and get those cuts seen to."

The five guards walked slowly away eastwards, back towards the café.

Johnny waited and watched. After a couple of minutes, once the others had gone around a slight bend on the beach, Ed stood up, switched his torch on and walked to the edge of the rocks. He looked at his watch. It was low tide. The rocks between him and the three boxes were still covered with thousands of chocolate biscuit wrappers now mixed up with unravelled rolls of shiny white photographic paper washed ashore from the last tide.

Johnny continued to observe from the safety of his dark hiding place, as Ed started to pick his way carefully towards the boxes, his torch in one hand and what Johnny thought to be a blade of some sort, in the other.

He only managed to walk about two metres before he lost his balance completely. His feet shot up in front of him and the big man fell heavily backwards, his head hitting a rock as he splash landed on a bed of seaweed and plastic. Johnny watched him fall and was tempted to rush down and see if he was all right but instead, he stood dead still deciding what best to do next.

He quickly made a plan and dropped down onto the beach, put his jacket hood up to cover his face and ran over to the rocks. He slithered across to Ed and picked up his torch which had tumbled to the edge of the rock pool. Ed was out for the count. Johnny bent down, shone the torch at Ed's chest and put his ear close to his mouth. Thankfully his chest was moving and despite the noise of crashing waves breaking on the rocks nearby, he could just about hear him breathing. He'll be OK Johnny thought, but he was aware that the guard could recover consciousness at any moment. He had to act fast.

Johnny spotted the shiny object Ed had been carrying, it was indeed a hacksaw blade. Carefully, he slithered back to the beach then ran over to the green container - he wanted to see what Leo and Jack had been doing. He picked up one of the sawn through padlocks and noticed the other one had been almost cut through. He put a handkerchief around his hand, grasped the blade and continued to saw through the second lock. Within minutes he'd managed to cut right through it and the bars holding the door tightly closed were now able to be turned in such a way that sections of the big end door could be opened.

He did just that and peered inside with squinted eyes. His gaze was met by a stack of large cardboard boxes packed tightly one against the other. His hacksaw blade was soon busy cutting a hole in the side of one of the boxes. When it was big enough, he shone his torch inside and saw lots of black plastic bags about the size of normal kitchen bin bags. He pulled and tugged on one of them until it suddenly popped out, just like a cork from a bottle, almost causing him to lose his balance. He dropped the bag a couple of metres away from the door and still out of the security light cover, he unwound the long thin plastic strip which had been used to tie up the bag. He reached inside and pulled out a handful of the contents.

He gasped, swore and couldn't believe his eyes. No, this wasn't possible! This only happens in fictional pirate tales and on treasure islands. Johnny was clutching a bundle of Euro banknotes. There was a selection of €20 notes, €50 notes and €100 notes just in one small handful. There must be thousands of them, he guessed, in that one bag alone.

Off came his backpack and the booty was stuffed into every possible space both in the bag and the pockets of his clothes. He would have loved to go down and fill another bag but he simply couldn't carry any more and for all he knew, the replacement security guards could be right around the corner. Johnny picked up one of the plastic bags which was still about half full, slung it over his shoulder and after a quick glance at the still motionless Ed, set off back up the path. He didn't want to leave his bike at the church so he balanced the bag across the handlebars and rode carefully home.

Mum and Dad were out having a meal with friends and Leo was in the bath, probably nursing his cut legs. Johnny went into the garden room by the back door and emptied his pockets, the contents of his rucksack and the black plastic bag he was carrying onto the large table. In disbelief his fingers spaced out his amazing find. There must be hundreds of thousands of Euros here he thought with a broad grin on his face.

"I've got something for everybody here," he shouted up to Leo. "Come down and see!"

A minute or so later Leo appeared with a towel wrapped around his waist. He stared at the table which was covered with notes, then at Johnny and for the first time in his life he gave his younger brother the tightest hug he had ever had.

"Tell me I'm dreaming little brother, I've never, ever seen so much money!"

"Not a word to Mum and Dad, Johnny," he warned starkly, then he rubbed his hands together yelling, "Wey-hey! Come on you little looter, how did you get all that then?"

Two weeks later Dad drove Leo and Johnny to Honiton station to catch the Friday evening 6:59pm train to London, Waterloo. Leo told his Mum and Dad he was taking Johnny to see Tasha, their sister and her boyfriend Harry. They were going to stay in Tasha's flat and would probably all go into London on Saturday to do a bit of sightseeing and they'd return on Sunday afternoon.

However this wasn't the real plan.

On Saturday morning at 9.00am sharp, Leo picked up a hired car from a garage near his sister's flat and all four of them set off on a course to Dover. They caught the late morning ferry to Calais, then after the short crossing, Leo drove to a couple of French hypermarkets near the ferry terminal. By the end of the afternoon they were exhausted and overwhelmed and Leo drove back to the terminal and waited for the next ferry back to Dover. They were all feeling quite pleased with themselves and the car boot bulged with their new purchases.

Once all the vehicles were safely on board the ferry, they headed up on deck to watch it leave the port then went to the restaurant where everyone enjoyed a hearty meal. A few drinks followed in the bar as they watched the eclectic selection of programmes being shown on the large television screen. About half an hour before they were due to arrive in Dover, Leo visited the on board shop and bought a couple of bottles of single malt whiskey, one for his Dad and one for his Uncle, and a bottle of gin for his Mum. He also picked up a selection of huge chocolate bars and paid for them all with the last €100 note he'd brought with him.

Shortly afterwards there was an automated tannoy announcement requesting all car drivers to rejoin their vehicles and before too long they were driving off the boat toward the customs and passport check point. The long line of cars proceeded slowly and as Leo's vehicle approached the front of the queue, two officials approached the car, one stood in front of the bonnet, the other came around to the driver's window. He asked Leo to pull over and drive into the shed on the left. Concerned glances were exchanged by all.

The officials requested everyone to get out of the car and all of a sudden, they were surrounded by four customs officers, three male and one female.

"When did you all go to France?" one of the male officers asked Leo.

"This morning," Leo replied. "We went to do a bit of shopping near Calais."

"Where do you live?" the official asked.

Leo replied for them all. "I live with my parents and young brother Johnny in Branscombe in Devon and my sister lives with her partner in London."

"Could you open your car boot, please?" he said.

Leo did as he was told and the officers cast their eyes over bags and bags of groceries, bottles of wine, packs of lager and beer, some expensive top quality audio equipment and computer software. Draped over the back seats on the parcel shelf were even more plastic bags packed with new items of clothing and wedged between Tasha and Harry on the back seat were copious boxes of new shoes.

"Did you pay for all of these items by credit card?" the official asked.

They looked at one another.

"No, with cash," Leo replied.

"Do you have all the receipts?"

"Yes," said Leo.

The man continued his line of questioning in a monotone voice. "When you were on the boat just now did you purchase anything?"

"We had a meal, some drinks, then I bought a few things from the shop."

"Two bottles of whiskey, one bottle of gin and some bars of chocolate I understand," replied the customs officer.

Leo suddenly felt the blood drain from his face. "Yes, that's right," he stammered. His heart was now sinking down into his new boots.

"And did you pay cash?"

"Yes, yes, I did." Leo now began to feel as though he might be sick very soon.

"Can you remember the value of the note you used to pay for these items?"

"Yes, it was my last €100 note," he said softly, staring at the floor. He felt awful. Totally gutted.

"Correct!" said the officer, holding up a €100 note. "In fact this is the very note you used to purchase these items. You see, unluckily for you, the young French sales assistant being a vigilant sort of person noted the serial numbers on this high value note. They checked to see if they matched a list of stolen notes which they'd been issued a week or so ago and they matched perfectly. The reason she checked was simple, a mistake had been made when these €100 notes were printed. The last six digits were in fact letters not numbers and they caused a great deal of amusement at the time! If you've any knowledge of French," he continued, "I'm sure you'll agree the letters 'PPKAKA' are a little unusual."

With a weak smile Leo replied, "Yes, I've got it. I lived in France for a while with my family."

Johnny's startled expression caught the eye of the officer standing nearby and he leaned in towards him.

"Did you hear what my colleague said to your brother?" he enquired.

"Yes, I heard what he said and I know what the letters mean."

"Well young man," said the officer, "your little shopping spree across the Channel has just landed you in an awful lot of it!"

The first officer was still holding the note in his hand - he waved it at them.

"These out of circulation notes were on their way to a South African pulp mill on a container vessel called the Napoli. She ran aground off a Devon beach which coincidentally happens to have the same name as the village where two of you live."

The game was well and truly over. The four exchanged brief glances and Tasha started to cry. Harry put his arm around her shoulder to offer comfort.

"Would you all follow me into the office please," the officer continued, "and perhaps you could tell us precisely how this stolen €100 note came into your possession."

Leo, Johnny, Tasha and Harry entered the customs office followed by the female officer who quietly shut the door behind her.

Striker's Valley

"Well, it's all agreed then!" boomed Colonel Beeton as he stood by his big shiny car, in front of Branscombe Village Hall.

"Yes Colonel," said Betty Button, "We'll find out how much it would cost to fill in The Old Marsh and turn it into a car park."

High up, perched on a television aerial, Striker the buzzard eavesdropped on their brief conversation. For a long while he considered what to do next and how to tackle this big problem. It wasn't their marsh; they had no right to fill it in. How dare they! Before darkness descended, Striker launched himself into the grey evening sky and flapped up the valley to find Digger.

Yes, it was time for battle. Digger was a large badger who lived with his family deep underground, close to Squire's Lodge where the Colonel lived. Digger sniffed the evening air at the entrance to his home then with his nose to the ground he shuffled off along a well-worn track in search of food. He was looking for worms, grubs, and slugs or other tastier morsels to eat.

At the side of a tall beech tree, he stopped his foraging, raised his head and again sniffed the air. He stood on his back legs, stretched his limbs and cleaned and sharpened his claws against the bark of the tree. Feeling ever hungrier, he shuffled onto where the edge of the wood met the narrow lane leading to Squire's Lodge. He crossed the lane and crept under a tall hedge. Suddenly something grabbed one of his back feet and squeezed it tightly. Digger groaned with pain. He tried to twist around to see what it was that had grabbed him but each time he moved, a stabbing pain shot through his body.

"Ow!" Digger moaned. "Ow! Ow! Ow!"

High above, Striker heard Digger's feeble call for help and swooped down to where the sound had come from.

"Thank goodness you've come," Digger gasped. "Something has grabbed one of my back feet and I can't move."

Striker hopped over to investigate Digger's trapped foot.

"It's a snare," he said. "The Colonel uses them to catch rabbits. I've seen him carrying them back to his home."

"How can I get my foot out?" gasped Digger almost crying with the pain.

"I'll see what I can do," said Striker.

With one claw he held the snare and with his tough beak he carefully gripped the wire loop that was trapping Digger's foot.

"Ow! Ow! Ow!" Digger groaned again.

"Be brave," said Striker. "Be brave."

Striker pulled; very gently at first; then a bit harder, then a little harder, working at the wire again and again until the loop opened just wide enough to release poor Digger's foot.

From round the bend in the lane, headlights suddenly shone through the hedge immediately followed by the rush and roar of a car as it sped towards Squire's Lodge. Striker, surprised by the bright lights, flapped instinctively into the darkening sky whilst remembering to call out to his friend the reason for his mission:

"Meeting at The Old Marsh, next Full Moon."

Gerty was a goose. She was feeling fed up. She and all the other geese who lived at the Old Mill below Squire's Lodge were in their small shelter, locked up for the night, listening to the rain hammering down on the wooden roof.

They couldn't sleep outside at night because sneaky foxes sometimes crept up to their home at the bottom of the valley, near the stream in search of an evening meal. It had poured with rain all day. "When was it going to stop she wondered?" As evening passed into night time, she tucked her long white neck under her wing, closed her eyes and drifted off to sleep.

As dawn broke there was a loud clap of thunder, the sound of which seemed to bounce from side to side of the long valley. Gerty and all her friends woke with a start. Frightened by the loud noise, they all started to cackle as they shuffled and stumbled around their dark shelter. Gerty, by far the largest goose among them, was standing in a corner. The others looked upon her as their leader, mainly because of her size. All at once, following an even louder clap of thunder, they rushed over to be closer to her. The sudden weight of all these geese in one corner was too much for the elderly wooden goose house. Beneath their webbed feet, there was a splintering crack as two of the four wooden supports, which kept the shelter off the ground cracked and split open.

What happened next was nothing less than total chaos. One end of the shelter collapsed heavily onto the ground. All the geese slithered towards poor Gerty who was well and truly squashed by the weight of so many frightened companions. It was still pouring with rain and Gerty, whose large body was now being pressed against the ground, couldn't understand why dirty, rather smelly, water was starting to rise up all around her. "Where was all this water coming from?" She wondered.

"Quiet all of you!" she shrieked. And for a brief moment there was silence. "What's that roaring noise?" She said to the others. The answer came to her in a flash. Dark water seeping into the broken shelter, the sound of rushing water from the stream. "Oh no, oh no!" She gasped "NOT A FLOOD! If it keeps rising, we'll all be drowned!" Gerty knew about the danger of flood water because when she was a little gosling her best friend Gabby had been washed away in a storm, never to be seen again…

The mill owner was woken suddenly and jumped out of bed by the screeches of terror coming from his goose house.

"Not that fox again," He muttered to himself as he hastily pulled on his trousers. Grabbing a torch and his raincoat, he ran out into the storm and down towards the stream. Shining his torch in front of him he strode through the darkness, rain and flood water, towards the shelter. His boots, now almost full of water, kept getting stuck in the mud.

Just as he arrived at the broken shelter, he spotted another torchlight coming from the gate by the Mill Cottages. A neighbour was coming to help rescue his gaggle of geese. He, too, had been woken up by the terrible shrieking. The men grabbed some bricks, which were stacked up by the gate and with a one, two, three, they heaved the broken end of the shelter just high enough to place bricks underneath to offer temporary support. The shelter door was then opened and a flurry of feet and feathers flapped noisily into the dark. Gerty stood with flood water up to the top of her short legs. She shook herself, waggled her tail feathers, stretched her neck then waddled as fast as she could up the steep field followed closely by all the others.

As dawn approached and Gerty's world slowly began to get lighter and lighter, she looked at the effect of the flood. The narrow winding stream she knew so well, was now a wide rushing torrent of water. The wooden plank across the stream had gone and the large flat stone she used to drink from had also disappeared.

As the first rays of sun pierced the low mist trapped in the valley, the rain stopped. All through the morning the flood water slowly crept back towards the old watercourse. Later on the mill owner came back into the field and hammered two new supports under the shelter. The neighbour arrived and the repaired shelter was carried back to its usual flat site. Scrubbed out dishes were filled with food, the smell of which soon reached Gerty's nostrils. She tugged at some grass shoots then waddled after the others down to the shelter.

Before she bent down to eat the grain, Gerty heard a flapping sound and immediately spotted Striker perched on the end of the repaired shelter. "Gerty," he said, "meeting at The Old Marsh, next full moon."

Later that day, Striker was at the far end of the valley to make contact with the next member of his team.

Venom Viper was enjoying basking in the welcome sunshine after the storm. He lived on a sunny slope right in front of the valley's fruit and flower farm. Dotted about the slope were many large, flat stones on which he liked to sunbathe and feel the breeze and the warmth of the sun's rays caressing every part of his thin, cool body. He often used to hear the barks and the growls of the two farm dogs, Maddy, a black and white sheep dog, and Grippa, a large lumbering Bulldog, as they patrolled their territory warning everyone and everything that they were on guard. Whenever Venom heard them coming his way, he would quietly slither off into the long grass so that he wouldn't be seen. Most of the valley animals kept clear of Venom. Snakes, if surprised, were known to bite and kill so they were left alone. Venom, in fact, had never bitten anyone in anger. He considered himself to be a friendly snake who preferred to be on his own but he also felt that if someone or something should ever invade his space then he would probably become very angry.

That morning, under a clear, blue sky, Venom slid through the grass to one of his favourite stones in the middle of the orchard below the greenhouses. He curled up on the stone, closed his eyes and fell into a deep sleep. When he woke up he got the shock of his life. All he could see was the whiskery face and pointed ears of Maddy from the farm. Maddy had never seen a snake before and she didn't quite know what to make of this long, grey, zigzag patterned tail curled up in front of her. She made a few friendly whining noises hoping that this strange tail would start to wag like hers.

Venom stayed very still. Maddy seemed so big and threatening, standing there in front of him, casting her shadow over his warm body. Being an inquisitive dog, Maddy decided to take a closer look. Her cold, wet nose almost touched Venom's head. This was too close for comfort. Venom raised his head, arched his body and hissed sharply at the nosy dog.

Surprised and frightened, Maddy leapt backwards, all her four paws off the ground. With her ears flat to her head and her tail held tightly between her legs, she rushed off back towards the farm yelping as loudly as she could. Venom settled down again on his stone and closed his eyes. Not for long! The ground began to shake and Venom realised that something big and heavy was coming towards him at great speed. Before he had time to slither into the long grass, Grippa was there right in front of him, at first panting heavily, then snarling and growling aggressively. Large drops of slimy slobber dripped from his wet, floppy jaws.

This was too much for Venom. For the first time in his life he felt angry, really angry. His privacy had been invaded by this grotesque monster whose dripping jowls were making him wet and uncomfortable. Grippa had never been afraid of anything and this thing, whatever it was, which had frightened poor Maddy, was going to be taught a lesson. He jabbed his huge head down to bite Venom but he wasn't quick enough. Venom lunged forward, sunk his fangs into Grippa's paw, and vanished into the grass. Grippa let out a blood-curdling howl as the pain shot through his body. He licked his bitten paw vigorously, then howling with pain he hobbled back up to the farm.

Circling high above the farm, Striker had observed this noisy encounter so knew exactly where to find Venom. He spiralled down over Venom's stone and not wishing to interrupt him yet again, he called out, "Venom, meeting at The Old Marsh, next full moon."

A few days later, a large full moon started to rise in the sky over the valley. Word had got around and there in the middle of The Old Marsh on a small, raised, dry island carpeted with moss were gathered an assorted company of valley dwellers all keen to listen to Striker the Guardian of the Valley. All the valley animals called Striker their 'guardian' as he spent most of the day high in the sky watching over his territory, his valley just ten flaps away from The Jurassic Coast.

Striker told them all what the Colonel and others were planning and carefully explained the part that each one of them had to play in order to defeat the Colonel and his gang of marsh fillers.

"This marsh belongs to the valley," Striker pronounced "and this valley is our home. It provides us with food and shelter and has been untouched for hundreds of years. It must remain that way, so we have just over ten sunsets to make sure that our plan will succeed."

The sunsets passed and everyone was ready. That evening the Colonel arrived at the village hall in his car accompanied by Betty Button and two men whose job it would be to fill in The Old Marsh. Other people soon arrived and went inside to join the Colonel. Striker's team and reinforcements were all discreetly hidden nearby. They were all ready to put their carefully timed plan into action.

Digger's role in the plan had been to assemble a night-time team of badgers to dig rows of wide linked tunnels close to the surface next to the small existing car park. The evening before, Digger's tall, strong friend, Hercules Heron had managed to find the one above ground water tap and had turned it on just after the Colonel arrived. Within minutes all of the tunnels were full of water.

Just after 8 o'clock, everyone came outside to look at and to discuss what had to be done to The Old Marsh. They walked past their cars straight into their first unpleasant surprise.

Within seconds, there was a lot of shrieking and shouting as the combined weight of their bodies made the ground above the tunnels collapse. The marsh 'thieves' struggled to clamber out of the cold, water filled, crumbling trenches. Shoes were lost and clothes were covered in mud as they helplessly lurched from one collapsing tunnel to another.

Overhead, Hercules and a squadron of herons appeared and large beach pebbles rained down on all the unfortunate victims. Some pebbles missed their target but others scored direct hits. The Colonel had his expensive new hat knocked off and, in her panic to get away from this horrible place, Betty Button's new shoes became well and truly stuck in the mud.

"The back door! Everyone head for the back door!" yelled the Colonel as his bedraggled friends desperately made for shelter. As they struggled through the back door, each one trying to get in before the other, they met the next horror. There on the floor Venom and forty-nine other snakes squiggled and squirmed all over the place. In one synchronised move, all the snakes started to slither towards the horrified cluster of mud-splattered humans, bunched together just inside the back door entrance. Bodies pushed, pulled and kicked as they desperately tried to eject themselves in whatever way possible out into the open again. Those who succeeded headed for the safety of the wide reception area at the front of the hall.

As the Colonel flung the doors open, Gerty Goose and her friends appeared from the far side of the hall. They raised their heads high and screeching and cackling at full volume, they pursued the humans into the hall.

This was the final straw for Betty Button who promptly fainted and collapsed. Three people tried to help her up but couldn't because Gerty and her followers were constantly pecking at their legs and bottoms.

In a scene of total chaos, mud, water, discarded clothing, cuts and bruises, tears, screeches and shouts, the humans hurried back out towards their cars dented by beach pebbles. Car engines roared into life and the battered vehicles and their frightened occupants zoomed off in search of safety.

Job done, mission accomplished! Striker's team quietly left for their homes under a gradually darkening night sky.

Several days later a large typed announcement was placed by Betty Button on the village Notice Board for all to see. It simply said,

MARSH CAR PARK PLAN ABANDONED. Signed: Colonel I.M. Beeton.

Captain McClonkey's Cabin

On the harbourside in the busy Devon port of Exmouth, squeezed between two old grey warehouses, was a brightly painted little wooden cabin. Over the front door the words 'MA WEE HOOSE' were written on a polished name plate and for only a few weeks of the year, this humble cabin with an old ship's bell hanging from a long rope beside the front door; was the home of Captain Jock McTavish McClonkey. Captain Jock came to Exmouth from Scotland many years ago. As a young man he loved fast motor bikes but most of all he really loved searching for all sorts of fossils so The Jurassic Coast was just the place for him.

On his fifteenth birthday he went to sea for the first time and there wasn't an ocean or a sea he hadn't chugged across during his fifty years travelling the world. One January evening, off the west coast of France, great big waves rolled his rusty old boat and he made up his mind that this was going to be his last voyage. Never again would he put to sea, never again would he have to face the ocean's temper and the long months away from his comfy cabin.

"Aye!" he said to himself as he clung on to the ship's wheel,

"I'm goin' ta retire ta ma wee hoose an' I'm goin' ta spend all ma time ridin' ma big bike an' lookin' for big fossils on the beach."

Meanwhile, back in Exmouth, Captain McClonkey's cabin was alive with activity. Hidden in the woodwork was an unbelievable collection of creepy crawlies that would soon present poor old Jock with the worst retirement present you could possibly imagine. From the time when his grandfather Alistair McTavish McClonkey lived in the cabin, millions and millions of ants, beetles, spiders, worms and cockroaches had scratched, bored, burrowed and bitten their way into the cabin's floors, walls, ceilings and roof. Some of them had come from the town, some from the countryside and many a creepy crawly from faraway lands had scuttled out of wooden crates stored in the old warehouses on either side of Captain McClonkey's cabin into the safety of his home.

In every room, huge families of fat bugs of all shapes and sizes, some with wings, some without, munched and munched, then slept, then munched again year in and year out until they could eat no more. The cabin provided them with all the food they could ever need WOOD! WOOD! WOOD! Layer upon layer of lovely, tasty… wood.

After generations of munching and crunching and chomping and chewing all over poor old Captain McClonkey's cabin, every part of its wooden frame was gradually becoming weaker and weaker. To make matters worse every bit of furniture made of wood such as the Captain's table, chairs, bed, and bookcase had all been attacked and devoured by hordes of woodworm. They had transferred their home from crates of Scottish Whisky stored in the warehouse to old Jock's cabin.

The little cabin contained yet another surprise. If you looked into the corners of the living room, you would see the sagging webs made by 'Gargantula' a huge cable spinning spider whose real home was far away from Exmouth deep in the dark damp forests found in parts of the continent of South America. She had arrived, by accident, in a crate of bananas many years ago and looking for somewhere quiet and sheltered, had scuttled over to the calm of the McClonkey cabin. The weight of her gigantic webs was now so great that the corners of the living room were slowly beginning to lean inwards.

Back on the bridge of his battered old boat, practising strange sounds on his dusty tartan bagpipes, happy Captain Jock chugged into warm and sunny Exmouth. Alongside the harbour wall he tied up his faithful old boat for the very last time. He picked up his bags and his bagpipes and walked across the cobbled quayside to his home. He opened the door, dropped his belongings in the kitchen then went straight out to the little shed in his backyard where he kept his powerful gleaming red and silver motorbike. He put on a shiny black crash helmet, checked the petrol, kick started the big engine that roared into life and within minutes he was racing out of Exmouth towards the wild open countryside of Dartmoor. No more waves, no more rolling around from side to side, just good solid Devon earth beneath his speeding wheels. For hours he raced across moorland tracks and roads, scaring the wool off the sheep, scattering the ponies in all directions, frightening the pants off roadside hikers and waking anybody who might have dozed off in the warm summer sunshine of this lovely day.

Just before tea time, Jock screeched to a halt outside his home, wheeled his hot machine into the shed, hung up his helmet, turned the key in the padlock and walked across the little yard to his back door. In the living room, the floor and all the furniture was covered in a thick blanket of fine dust. His nose immediately started to twitch. He spotted his favourite old saggy leather armchair and promptly flopped down into it. As his backside hit the cushion, a great cloud of grey and white dust rose upwards towards the ceiling. Full of fresh air from his mad dash over the moor, the Captain yawned, closed his eyes then nodded off to sleep. As he snored, the cloud of powdery dust gently drifted down from the ceiling. His long nose sucked in vast quantities that tickled and teased the hairs of his nostrils. With his mouth wide open the Captain snorted like a happy piglet. Every now and then he would hastily wipe his itchy nose with the dusty sleeve of his jacket. Jerking his head backwards, he took in one enormous breath then, as if someone was tickling him all over, his whole body started to shake. All of a sudden, with mouth wide open, he let rip three of the most deafening sneezes you have ever heard in your life,

"A-A-A-A-A- A" CHOO! once

"A-A-A-A-A- A" CHOO! twice and

"A-A-A-A-A- A" CHOO! thrice.

The sound of these thundering sneezes bounced from wall to wall then from floor to ceiling before bursting into the bedroom, the bathroom and finally the kitchen. Then there was silence. Very slowly at first, the cabin started to tremble, just a little, then the tremble turned into a wobble, then a shake, just like a jelly sitting on a plate.

High up in the corner of the living room Gargantula frightened by this unusual explosion of sound hastily 'clank, clank, clanked' her way from one side of her cable web to the other. Behind her the wall creaked then groaned as it started to move inwards. Poor old Captain Jock's retirement surprise, was about to commence. The wall continued to creak and lean, and lean until 'BANG' it all collapsed onto the floor showering old nails and splinters everywhere. Within seconds it was followed by another crumbling wall, then another, then another, then with the walls gone the ceiling moaned, creaked loudly, and then crashed down onto the ground, one or two bits bouncing off the Captain's thatch of grey hair as they plummeted down onto him. The same thing happened in the other three rooms, one after the other. Again from above with sounds like a volley of gun shots the cabin roof timbers split, cracked then collapsed. Chunks of rotten wood rained down past poor old Captain Jock hitting the ground with a thud then, as if by magic, bursting into showers of splinters and dust.

A few minutes later after the last wooden missile had bounced off his now bruised and aching head, Captain Jock rose from his tattered chair. Under a powdery veil he looked like a monster. Covered in dust from the top of his head to the soles of his boots, he gazed around in disbelief at the shattered remains of his lovely little home. He fumbled his way over to the place where his front door used to be, tripped over the large bell that used to hang alongside, and fell head first into the carpet of debris and dust. He uttered a few well chosen rude words; sat up; and remained motionless, not knowing what to do next.

Without realising what he was doing, he bent over and started to scratch his ankles, then up his shins to his knees. He quickly stood up and continued scratching with both hands, higher and higher, under his belt, around his waist, up to his chest, his neck, in fact all the way up to his hair.

The sound of his collapsing cabin and the clouds of dust hanging in the air above the quayside drew a large crowd, curious to see what had just happened. Within minutes everyone started scratching their necks, hair, arms and legs and nearby Captain Jock was seen jumping up and down shouting

"OOCH! OOCH! SHOO YA BEASTY! SHOO SHOO YA BEASTY!"

as he frantically slapped his dusty clothes. Then, with his boots clattering along the cobbles of the harbour he was last seen leaping around in circles that got wider and wider, being chased by furious bugs and a very angry spider!

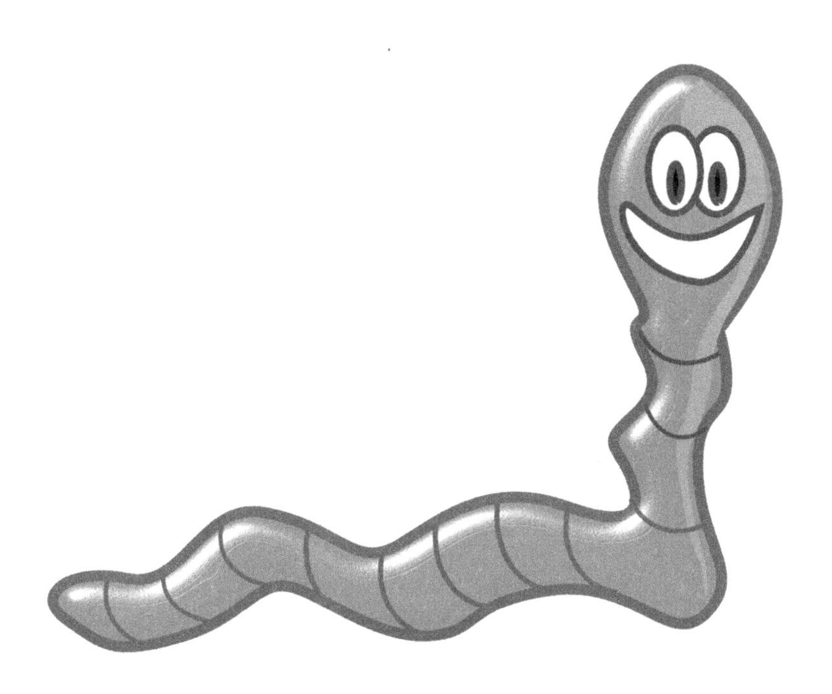

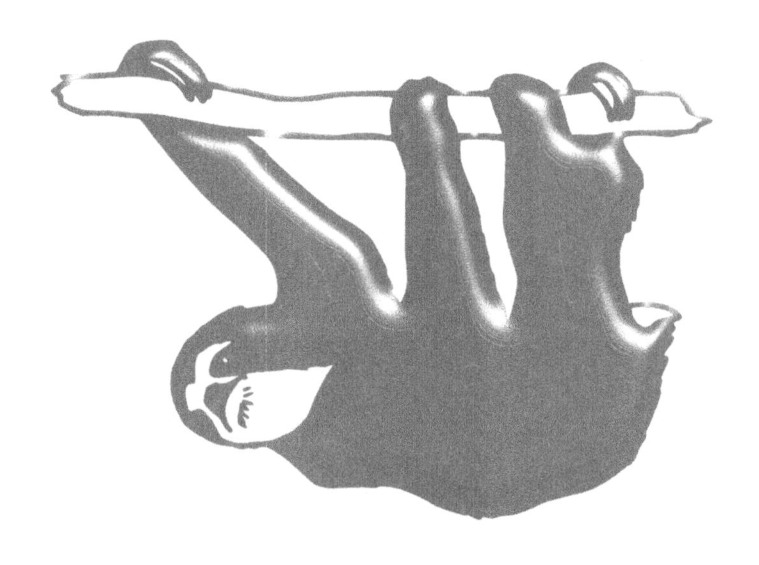

Joath the Sloth

In the delightful Dorset coastal village of Dibbledowndelly you could feel the buzz of excitement as the big day began.

At precisely midday the big bell would ring to start the Dibbledowndelly 'DASH' a race open to anyone or anything that could walk, creep, crawl, shuffle, stumble, slink, wriggle, slither or slide their way from the starting line of the race track to the finish.

Joath the Sloth had been training for this big day for a long while and at last, he felt ready to race. He normally felt more relaxed at home, up in the trees, hanging out with his friends. But finally, after weeks and weeks of walking practice on his three-toed feet and with the help of two long stout sticks he was ready to go.

The Sloths in the village of Dibbledowndelly were known to be so slow, so amazingly, incredibly, annoyingly slow in whatever they did so by the rules of this race, he was in with a chance!

However, there was one creature in the Dibbledowndelly 'DASH' whom Joath the Sloth would find very hard to beat.

Dug the Slug was the 'DASH' Champion. He had been the Champion for years and years, as no one could beat him. This was a big challenge for Joath who had made up his mind that this year he was going to beat Dug. It wasn't speed he had trained for, just the opposite. He had trained to go slower and slower for hours and hours without stopping.

What sort of race was the Dibbledowndelly 'DASH'? Well, it was a race unlike any other and the rules were very simple. The winner was the person or creature who would take the longest time to go from the

Starting Line to the Losing Line. Anyone who could walk normally on two legs would complete the race distance in about one minute but for all those who typically signed up for the 'DASH' they would take much, much longer.

Joath the Sloth was tall, very hairy and much thinner than he normally was after weeks of hard training, whilst his arch rival Dug the Slug was small, smooth and fat.

Everyone knew that this year's winner would be either Dug the Slug, once again, or the new contender, Joath the Sloth. There were many other creatures who were taking part in the 'DASH' but they always reached the Losing Line far too early so they didn't really count.

At midday all the competitors were lined up ready to go. The big bell rang to announce the startof the race and they were off. The pace was slow, unbelievably slow and after a minute or two most of the spectators had wandered off to do something else.

After one hour Joath the Sloth felt fine, most of the other competitors had gone ahead and, as expected, it was just him and Dug the Slug left to battle it out.

After two hours Joath the Sloth was starting to feel a bit uncomfortable. His feet and toes were aching and although admired for his slowness, he had never, ever, moved so slowly in all his life as he was doing now. It was going to be tough to beat Dug the Slug.

After three hours poor old Joath the Sloth was in a great deal of pain, but he wasn't going to give up and race ahead to the Losing Line. He held on tightly to his two stout sticks and very, very slowly shuffled along dragging one foot after the other.

Dug the Slug, as usual, seemed very happy with his pace. He knew that he was going to win; he was; after all, the reigning champion.

Joath the Sloth stared at Dug the Slug and felt sure that he wasn't moving at all. Stopping at any point in the 'DASH' was totally forbidden, but crafty old Dug knew what he was doing.

After four hours Joath the Sloth was on the point of saying "Ok, you win, you are the champion and without doubt the slowest creature in the village!" but, all of a sudden things changed.

Someone had spilled some juice on the track. Now Dug the Slug had two passions in his life, one was slurping up tasty sweet juices and the other was dancing with his girlfriend, Silvia Snail.

As Dug slurped up the juice on the track he started to dream about slithering and sliding around the dance floor with slippery Silvia. A sluggy smile crept across his face and he felt a burst of energy as he snuggled up to Silvia. Oh, what a dream! What a lovely dream!

Dug had completely forgotten what he was doing and in his excitement he had started to move faster. He was slipping and sliding and slithering with his beloved Silvia. He was in a different world, lost in his dreams.

Joath the Sloth noticed this unexpected burst of speed from his rival and couldn't believe his eyes. "Keep going like that Dug," he kept muttering to himself "keep going you slippery old slug".

After five hours most of the spectators had returned to the track to see the thrilling end of the race.

Poor old Joath was grasping his two sticks so tightly now and using all his strength just to keep standing up. His family, friends and most of the spectators were all shouting "Go slower Joath, go slower, you're almost there, don't stop, don't stop, keep on going!"

Meanwhile, fat Dug suddenly heard the big bell ring again to announce another racing loser as he slithered over the Losing Line. Because of his lapse in concentration during his dream of dancing with slippery Silvia, he'd forgotten all about the race! The reigning champion had just lost the 'DASH'!

A happy Joath shuffled over the Losing Line in tremendous pain, but the last competitor and the new race champion. Soon afterwards it was announced that this year's Dibbledowndelly Dash was the slowest ever on record.

Spectators had their photographs taken with the hairy victor. Everyone clapped, cheered and congratulated an exhausted Joath the Sloth, proudly wearing the champion's yellow scarf around his neck.

But what of Dug? Somehow in all the post-race excitement he simply vanished... he probably hadn't gone very far but the sad thing is, he was never seen again.

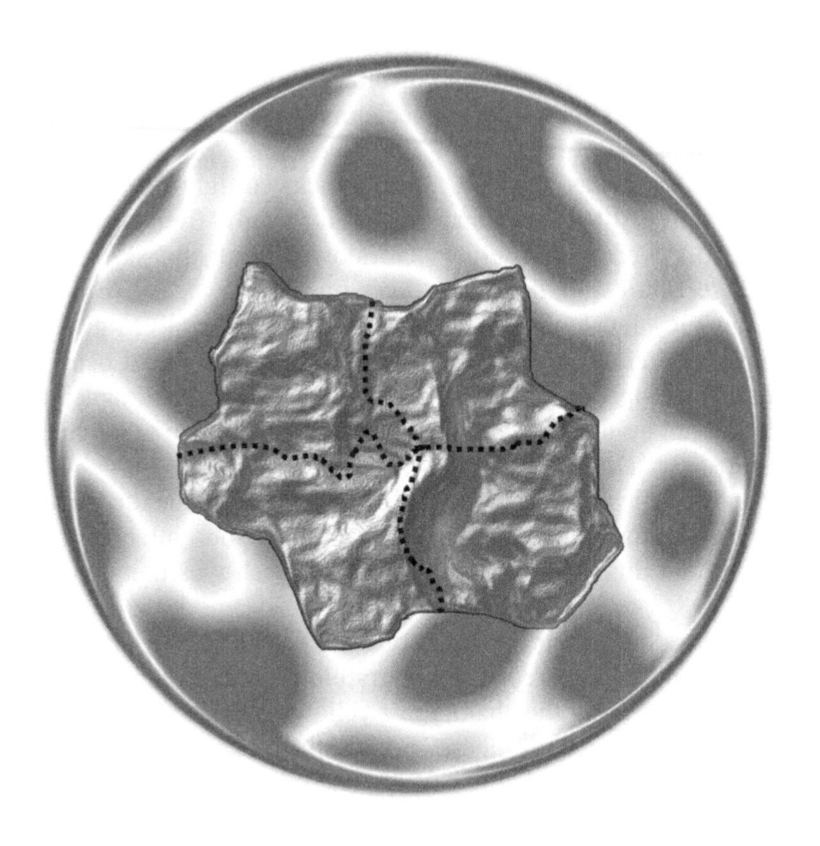

Astraflop

Introduction

Through a very good telescope you can just about see it; a small bright white blob; millions and millions of kilometres above planet Earth. This blob is, in fact, another planet called Terra and in the middle of a gigantic ocean on this planet is the huge island of Jurassica. The land on Jurassica is equally divided into four Quadrants. These Quadrants are called Terrasnotta, Terrablotta, Terraswotta and Terraposha. This island is unique. There are no other islands like it on Terra. In fact, Jurassica is the only island on the whole planet!

Right in the middle of the island, where the boundaries of these four Quadrants meet, is The Round House. This house is a large, circular building which serves as the 'Terrament' or meeting place where the leaders of the four Quadrants gather to discuss and prepare the Jurassica Journal, a newspaper which is distributed once a month to everyone on the island to tell them what they should know about new laws and regulations concerning the environment and education, also the latest gossip, photos and quadrant news, together with weather forecasts, several pages of adverts and all manner of ideas and events to help make everyone's life more enjoyable.

The Quadrant of Terrasnotta

What are the people like who live in this Quadrant? Well firstly, the inhabitants or 'Snottos' own and work the land, which covers the north-eastern part of the island. They consist mainly of friendly, hard-working farmers with round faces and large noses. They are also quite small in size but tough, and always determined to farm their huge fields as productively as possible.

In these huge fields bogey grass is grown. Acres and acres of bright green grass that is harvested twice a year then crushed into fine green flour. This green flour is mixed with snot oil, extracted from the stalks of the grass and then hand moulded into large balls. These large green balls are used in the preparation of bogey cakes, the staple diet of the Snottos. To prepare these bogey cakes, the green balls are cut into slices, then fried and served with a variety of vegetables.

Children particularly love these bogey balls not only to eat, but to play with. As a special treat for their children, Snotto parents divide a large bogey ball into dozens of tiny marble-sized green balls and bake them for thirty minutes. The resulting hard, shiny green 'bogeys' are used in a competitive game to see who has the hardest bogey, which can smash all the others into bits. However, the Snottos do have one little problem, which unfortunately affects most of the population. When they get excited, little droplets of water tend to drip from their large noses so they always carry a couple of ultra-absorbent hankies, just in case. This is particularly noticeable at football matches when emotions are running high.

Once a year, there is always a very exciting match between the two best teams in the Quadrant, Snotball United and Bogey City. One could imagine that if hankies were banned from the football stadium during the match, then hundreds of litres of nose water would have dripped onto the seats, onto other people's clothes, and onto the ground, making things most uncomfortable and unpleasant.

Snottos love television and the programmes which are the most popular are about cooking. They love to watch cookery demonstrations of exciting, tasty dishes which can be made with their favourite ingredients - bogey balls and bogey flour. The most popular cookery show of them all is presented by the young, attractive TV cook, Melanose Droppa. Apart from her wonderful dishes using local produce she, and other favourite chefs, frequently teach the population how to make the most of the not quite so important crops grown throughout the other Quadrants, along with a variety of simple meat dishes for the 'meatatarians' whom for many reasons prefer not to eat food made with bogey grass or cooked with snot oil.

Apart from watching television and trying out new recipes, many Snottos, both male and female, practise the unusual sport of grass knitting. This activity dates back to the time when after a very bountiful bogey grass harvest, some of the crop was put to one side. Then whilst the men on the farm made bogey flour and extracted snot oil, the women would carefully weave the long grass into hangings for their walls, windows, and carpets to put on the floors of the farm kitchens. They would also weave thick blankets to throw over their beds and some for animals when they were cold or sick. Many years ago there was a race between the women of two rival farms to see who could weave the longest grass scarf in one hour. Bit by bit, this nimble activity became more and more competitive. Men started to take part and nowadays, it is regarded as an important sport with teams all across the Quadrant. There are men's teams, women's teams, and even mixed teams seeing how well and how fast they can weave all sorts of wonderful creative things out of bogey grass.

Last year, Sebastian Smudge who worked on Long Wetnose Farm, (one of the most important bogey grass farms in the Quadrant) became quite a hero among the young males who took part in this unusual sport. For months he boasted that during the next annual Grass Scarf Knitting Competition he would be, without any doubt, the Quadrant champion. So sure was he that he would knit the longest scarf anyone had ever seen, he spent weeks and weeks practising. Sebastian used all of his spare time improving his knitting speed so he could go faster and faster. He was confident that when the three-day competition in June was announced he would be ready to take on anybody.

He had to be really good because the overall champion for the last four years, Semolina Quickneedle, was considered to be unbeatable. She, like Sebastian, when knitting at full speed could take your breath away. Her short, powerful fingers; like parts of a well-oiled machine; could produce an endless flow of yellowy-green, lightly woven, but amazingly soft scarves always to the exact width that was required.

On the first day of the competition very early in morning they started to knit, sitting in different rooms of the Round House, supported by friends and watched over by two judges. The seemingly endless supply of grass was passed along to Sebastian by his two best friends, Elliot Longleaf and Maxi Millfield whilst another two friends, Morwenna Mulch and Rosanna Roundroot kept him amply supplied with Bogey cakes and Boga Cola. In the next room to Sebastian, Semolina Quickneedle was similarly fed metres and metres of fine grass by her two friends, Louisa Lumpy and Amelia Spatchcock whilst a further two friends, Roberta Donkey and Anna Lisa Longbottom kept her well supplied with her favourite bogey biscuits and large mugs of herbal bogey tea.

By the end of day two they had both knitted twenty metres of scarf, which was continually rolled up into a scarf ball to keep it out of everyone's way.

On the third day, with just one hour of competition time left, everyone in the competition rooms was cheering on the two furiously knitting competitors. Their progress had been regularly reported on radio and television and the Quadrant's males were eagerly awaiting their first ever victory. With only ten minutes to go, both competitors had knitted an amazing thirty-two metres of scarf each. After another tense five minutes there was a sudden 'CRACK,' and cries of "Oh No! I don't believe it!" One of Sebastian's special competition needles had snapped. What a great panic there was! He had to stop for just a few seconds to replace his needle, then he did his very best to regain his knitting speed but, unfortunately, as the buzzer sounded to the end of the race, he knew that he had lost. Precise final measurements were taken before the ladies shrieked with joy as Semolina, for the fifth year in a row, had won by just one centimetre. Poor old Sebastian was heartbroken. If only that needle had lasted just five minutes longer, he and all his friends felt absolutely sure that he would now be wearing the large Grass Crown and not his rival, Semolina. Better luck next year!

The Quadrant of Terrablotta

Now, let's move on to Terrablotta, the south-eastern Quadrant situated below Terrasnotta. This Quadrant's inhabitants, known as the 'Blottos' are taller than the Snottos, and frequently a little absent-minded or forgetful, even confused at times. This slight problem of theirs sometimes leads to misunderstandings and an impression that for much of the time they aren't quite as friendly as their northern neighbours. However, like the Snottos they are basically a community of farmers who grow vast quantities of bogberries on the damp boggy marshes throughout the Quadrant. This south-eastern land is much wetter than the north, with many rivers snaking down into Terrablotta from the long mountain ranges, which separate each of the four Quadrants.

On the drier slopes of these mountains, Terrablotta farmers also grow snowberries and these together with the much larger crop of bogberries, are harvested twice a year and made into wine. From the red bogberries a sweet, red wine is produced in various strengths and similarly a drier white wine is produced from the mountain snowberries. The finest and most expensive Bogberry Red was produced in an old stone castle or 'Château' belonging to the well-known Brush family and a rare 1990 bottle of Château Bogbrush would cost a fortune to buy.

As the Blottos grow older their faces, particularly the men's faces, seem to get redder and redder, as if they have been out in the sun for too long. It is also very noticeable that elderly people in Terrablotta, more than in any other Quadrant, are seen to be stumbling around clutching walking sticks as if their legs were beginning to fail them. It has often been suggested by people from the other Quadrants that the Blottos drank too much and that this was the cause of their red faces and wobbly legs. The Blottos, of course, think that this suggestion is ridiculous, most unfair, rude and completely wrong.

Television, as in the other Quadrants is an important part of daily life with quizzes and game shows being the most popular. The programme, which always attracts the largest number of viewers every Saturday and Wednesday evening, is 'Lottoguess.' For this game you need a blank lotto or bingo card with sixteen empty spaces, which you have to fill with numbers. A selection of numbers, ranging from one to a hundred, are announced by well-known TV personalities and the viewer has to decide which numbers could be winners. They put their sixteen chosen numbers on the card then send it to the 'Lottocheck' to see if they have won. Many Blottos win big money prizes and occasionally there are 'rollovers' meaning even bigger sums of money could be won next time round if nobody guessed correctly that week.

Apart from playing 'Lottoguess' and appreciating good wine, the majority of Blottos are interested in sport and the one sport they play particularly well is Stilt Running. This sport has been practised in Terrablotta for hundreds of years and it started like grass knitting in Terrasnotta, as a friendly competition between big farms. The berry pickers collect the red bogberries and put them into large baskets strapped to their backs and as they tramped across the wide berry swamps, on stilts, they would race each other for fun. During the days when the berry pickers were not working, they would race one another on stilts across the wetlands and gradually, this bit of fun turned into a serious competitive sport.

About fifty years ago, a young Blotto called Cade Brownfield, the son of the farmer who owned the largest Bogberry Farm in Terrablotta, disappeared one day whilst trying to cross a very dangerous section of swamp on his stilts. His broken stilts were found months later but he was never found. This area, now known as 'Dead Man's Dump,' was left alone until only a few months ago when a similar event almost happened again.

South Blott Farm, famous throughout the Quadrant for its smooth, fruity red wine, housed about ten farm workers who worked on the farm all through the year. One Saturday evening two of these farm workers, Barnaby Bunge and Casper Cudmore, decided that they would attempt to cross Dead Man's Dump to prove their bravery to their workmates and friends. It was mid-summer and at that time of the year in Terrablotta it doesn't get dark until after midnight.

They set off at about six o'clock in the evening without telling their friends where they were going. After strapping on their long stilts they headed for the swamp and aimed for the nearest farm about three miles away. For the first couple of hours everything went well. The sky was clear and blue and they were warm under the evening sun. They laughed and joked as they plodded through the murky water of this vast swamp and wondered why other Blottos had a problem with this place. An hour or so later and about half way across they stopped, looked all around and started to realise what an empty and very, very flat place this was. There was nothing but brown water everywhere and the occasional grassy mound which rose above an ocean of smelly liquid. No sounds could be heard and no buildings could be seen in any direction.

A little bit worried, now that their confidence had worn off; they hurried on in the direction of the slowly sinking sun to where they believed; the farm and safety would be found. Without a compass, however, they couldn't be sure. A slight wind stirred. Stilt walking is never safe in windy conditions, so they hoped and prayed that this fresh breeze wouldn't strengthen. Suddenly, they heard a strange sound like someone moaning. It got louder, then softer, and then stopped. Could it be a noise from somewhere carried on the wind? It started again - a horrible sound. They felt cold as their bodies shivered with fear and goose pimples spread across their arms and legs.

A frightening thought came to them both. Could this be the ghost of the young Blotto who disappeared in the swamp, a young man of their own age? Was he trying to frighten them or to warn them of something? They looked at one another – terrified - then hurried on as fast as the swamp would allow them. Dead Man's Dump was indeed the right name for this dreadful place. Suddenly, something moved quickly just below the water and at speed hurtled straight into one of Casper's stilts and tugged at it. Casper lost his balance and fell into the brown murky water. The thing; whatever it was; disappeared without a ripple. Casper was stuck. He couldn't move and Barnaby couldn't help him either. With great difficulty, Casper managed, with one hand, to undo the strap on his one good stilt, the other one having been broken when he fell. Barnaby rummaged in his pockets for his BlottoPhone that he was lucky enough to have with him, and called for help. Meanwhile, Casper unstrapped the broken stilt, stood up to his knees in the pongy water and wet from head to foot, waded to the nearest raised ground where he flopped down on the scratchy grass and examined his broken stilt. Barnaby followed him. Casper passed the broken stilt up to Barnaby without saying a word. They looked at one another, both unable to speak, choked with fear. The stilt hadn't just snapped with the fall, around the splintered break there were teeth marks, big teeth marks. Casper drew his wet legs up onto the mound and Barnaby scanned the horizon, looking for any slight ripples in the flat, calm water.

Daylight was beginning to fade and it was getting noticeably cooler. The wind had dropped but Casper, hunched on the damp mound, started to shiver with fear, shock and cold. Soon night started to close in as the daylight ebbed away. Would they be the next two victims of Dead Man's Dump? Would whatever it was that bit and snapped Casper's stilt come back to finish them off? Was it watching them now, just waiting for the right moment to attack?

"Listen!" shouted Barnaby, "I can hear something."

Sure enough the air started to throb with the sound of an approaching blottocopter. They saw its lights, they waved and waved and within less than an hour they were back at the farm, no bones broken, a bit bruised but safe and warm with a hot drink in their hands. They told their amazing tale to their friends. "The beast of the swamp nearly had us," said Casper. "I now know why Cade was never found."

The Quadrant of Terraposha

Enough of the Blottos for the moment, let's move westwards across the dividing mountain range to the Quadrant of Terraposha where the Poshos live. The people who live in this Quadrant are very, very different to the Snottos and the Blottos. For a start they are very tall and slim. So tall that the Snottos and Blottos always feel that they are being looked down upon. They walk with slow measured steps, never appearing to be in a hurry. Poshos are always beautifully dressed; including their children; in well-cut, expensive looking clothes and unlike the hard-working farmers of the north and south-eastern Quadrants these south-western people seem to work much less and have much more time to do other things.

They are a private nation of people who, for most of the time, prefer their own company and only send a few senior members of their society to the Inter Quadrant meetings at the Round House. They don't produce special wines or green flour but they do manufacture, on a large scale, their own motorcar. This car is made by the Posho Motor Works and everyone seems to be driving around on their excellent roads in their brand new PMWs.

Posho's sport of choice is, of course, motor racing, keenly followed by the population, both on television and live at their three well designed race courses. Each track allows drivers to test their skills, the most difficult one being situated in the mountains bordering onto Terrablotta. There are many different types of PMWs all prepared for different types of races: Formula F races on the flat course, Formula M races in the mountains and the one the younger generation of Poshos really love, the Formula HS, a high-speed race on long beaches of hard sand.

The shops in Terraposha are full of lovely things. The towns and villages are always neat and tidy. Their seaside holiday resorts are full of large colourful hotels with extensive well-cared for gardens and terraces leading to swimming pools and jacuzzis of all shapes and sizes.

The television programmes preferred by most Poshos (apart from motor racing) are not quizzes, game shows or cookery demonstrations, but fashion programmes. Hours and hours of programmes informing the viewers of the very latest in styles, colours, fabrics, homewares, garden accessories and the most fashionable places to spend their next holiday. Where do they get the money to pay for all these things?

There are many in the other three Quadrants who are very suspicious of the Poshos. Questions are often asked as to how they have become so much richer than everyone else. There are all sorts of suggestions and theories as to how this may have happened but no real answer to that question has ever been given. They just seem to be... different from everyone else. Even the way they talk seems weird. Although all those who live in the four Quadrants speak the same language the Poshos speak very quickly, in short bursts, with rather a high pitched voice and frequently don't listen or care about what others are saying. They prefer their own company and clearly they are not liked very much by those who live beyond their mountain ranges. As long as they are able to lead their expensive life style, they couldn't really care less about anyone else.

However, there are occasions when the inhabitants of each Quadrant do; for various reasons; cross over the borders either North, South, East or West into the other Quadrants and yesterday on 'Radio Poshtalk,'- a telephone chat show- Marcus Electa, the snooty presenter, was listening to a very angry Blotto who was saying exactly what he thought about some of the young men in Terraposha. The reason why he was so angry was because the day before he had been delivering some bogberry and snowberry wine to a Posh Wine Shop not far from the border, when two young Poshos raced around a corner, far too fast in their PMW. They carelessly crossed over the white line in the middle of the road, very nearly hitting the Blotto coming the other way in his van. The Blotto braked hard to avoid them, skidded to a halt along the edge of the road, fortunately not hitting anything or anyone but inside the van six crates of wine had banged into each other breaking most of the bottles. Wine and broken glass spread out all over the back of his van as he was unable to clear up the mess. In his angry state, he immediately turned round and drove his rattly old van as fast as he could back towards the border hoping to catch up with the culprits.

The van, of course, was no match against a PMW, but Arthur Bottleby, the angry Blotto, had good eyesight and a very good memory. In the instant that he swerved his van out of the way of the PMW, he had caught sight of the registration plate and remembered it. Just before the border, Arthur spotted the PMW parked along with many others outside a 'PB' (Posh Bar). He stopped, got out and then headed for the door. Inside there was a lot of high-pitched chatter and screams of laughter around the tables where young Poshos were relaxing. Arthur cleared his throat, "Excuse me!" he shouted. Eyes turned towards him, frowned and the place went quiet. "Somebody here with a registration AM1POSH has a dent on their front wing." People drew in breath and looked at one another. Two young Poshos; Rupert Fortune and Tarquin Dollar; stood up and made their way to the door.

Arthur had by now left the building and was walking over to his van. Rupert and Tarquin followed him. Arthur was shorter than both the young Poshos and much older, but well known in Terrablotta as a respected boxing instructor.

"Well," said Rupert, "the wing on my car looks perfectly all right to me. I can't see any dent on it, can you Tarquin?"

"No, I can't," Tarquin replied smiling at his friend. "So what's all the fuss about, old man?"

Those last words were the last straw for Arthur. He stepped forward towards the two Poshos and very quickly grabbed hold of Rupert's left ear and Tarquin's right ear. He pulled Rupert's head sharply out to the left and Tarquin's head sharply out to the right, then very briskly BANGED both heads together.

"That's what it's all about my two pathetic Poshos. A little punishment for bad driving and for breaking my wine bottles."

Rupert and Tarquin were in pain. Arthur's head banging had hurt them more than they had ever experienced pain in their life. They walked around the 'PB' car park holding their heads in their hands, whining and grumbling at Arthur who by now, had got back into his van and was on his way back home.

The Quadrant of Terraswotta

Across the mountains, we journey over to the fourth Quadrant of Terraswotta where the Swottos live in the north-west. They are not great farmers or particularly rich but they are very well educated and they pride themselves on this. They have wonderfully equipped schools, colleges and universities with thousands of jobs available to suit all abilities. Every young person is expected to work hard, pass many different exams, reach the highest grades and be a credit to their parents.

Children are expected to do homework from the age of four every night of the week, go to extra learning classes during part of their school holidays and generally, lead a very pressured life. If they are really bright they might make it to Swotbridge University, the best in the Quadrant whose motto is simply, 'Grade or Fade'.

On their small farms they grow a range of healthy crops to help the brain develop. They eat lots of 'sweafood' which is considered good for the brain but despite all their academic learning, they also love to play competitive sports and team games like swicket, swootball, swugby, swennis, swockey, swunning and of course swimming. They are keen swikiers on their winter mountain slopes and instead of owning PMWs, the favourite vehicles in Terraswotta are four-wheel drives for both taking the children to school and for tackling the challenging race circuits all over the Quadrant. Marathon swunning, in recent years, has become perhaps the most watched sport on television in Terraswotta and watched outdoors at the five City and Country twenty-six mile circuits.

They have more educational television stations than all the other Quadrants put together and the number of books available throughout the Quadrant is enormous. Apart from books, there are hundreds of magazines full of interesting articles and colourful photographs, all published and sold on either a weekly or monthly basis.

The main problem in Terraswotta is that the Swottos are very boring people and the main topic of parental conversation in pubs, clubs, and at parties is 'Education', what the children are doing or should be doing at school, what grades they have achieved, how much extra learning time they are putting into their weekly routine and just how much their children have learnt since their last meeting.

However, not every young person achieves the grades expected of them and that's where the trouble starts. The 'Fallouts' as they are known are young Swottos who have fallen out of the strict school system, and therefore have fallen out with their teachers and parents. The only friends they have are other Fallouts like them. They get into trouble, and are considered an embarrassment to the Quadrant. Many of these troublemakers have already left Terraswotta and have found jobs on the bogberry farms of neighbouring Terrablotta. Here they enjoy the physical work, a different lifestyle and feel much happier. For them it's goodbye to books, homework and arguments at home and hello to Bogburst, Snowfizz, Lottoguess and stilt running.

Unlike the Fallouts, those who have climbed to the top of the achievement ladder are well-rewarded both with money and many appearances on television programmes. The Marathon champions are just as highly respected as those who have been successful in every possible exam in all sorts of different subjects.

Competition is intense and every year one male or one female between the ages of sixteen and eighteen is crowned as the YSSY or 'Young Super Swot of the Year'. In order to achieve this much sought after title, the competitors have to perform brilliantly in a long list of both sport and academic tests. From the end of March the six-month competition is open to any young person who wants to take part.

Each candidate is challenged in seven sports of their choice plus seven academic tests, the contents of which they choose from a list of about twenty specialised subjects prepared by Foxbridge University. The winner is the young person considered by the 'SAC' (The Special Awards Committee) to have obtained the highest number of points in all of the fourteen tests. The maximum number of points awarded for each test is fifty, so after fourteen tests the maximum total mark would be seven hundred points. The fifty points in the sport tests are for games won, goals scored, swickets taken, timed distances covered, and tactics. For the academic tests, points are awarded for correct answers.

In early September, Andrew Winner, a seventeen year old high school student from the north of the Quadrant, had achieved a total of 643 points and Felicity Highmark, an eighteen year old high school student from the south of the Quadrant had achieved 645 points. They each had one test left to take. There were ten questions and both Andrew and Felicity had answered the first nine correctly, earning a total of forty-five points each.

All that remained was the last question for five points when the one who got that right would be the overall champion, the Young Super Swot of the Year. Question ten was a verbal question read to them by a test judge whose job it was to make sure that there was no cheating. They both sat very still, looking at the judge and prepared themselves. No swalculators were allowed.

"Question number ten," said the judge.

He allowed ten seconds for calculation and then asked each candidate for their answer. Whoever got it right, then that was the end of the contest. If they both got it wrong, then he would repeat the question until one candidate eventually came up with the right answer. If they both got it right then he would ask a more difficult question to extend their brainpower. If the second question was answered correctly by both candidates then from the third question onwards the calculation would become more and more difficult. The nail biting competition was now against the clock so their hyperactive brains had to come up with the right answer very quickly.

"I want you to start with the number 17 then add 34, subtract 21, multiply by 7, add a further 325, divide by 5, then double your last answer and finally deduct 43."

The two brains worked furiously for just under ten seconds then two answers were written down on the answer sheet in front of them.

"There can be no alterations to your written answer from now," said the judge.

The two young Swottos nodded and relaxed back in their seats.

"Andrew, your answer please?"

"171," he replied.

"Felicity your answer please?"

"161," she replied.

The judge smiled.

"The correct answer is 171. Well done Andrew, you now have a total of 693 points against Felicity's 690. By a margin of three points you have become this year's Young Super Swot."

Andrew shouted, "Yeah!" and punched the air with relief and excitement.

Felicity smiled sweetly and they hugged one another. During the last four years, the girls had beaten the boys by three to one so now it was three to the girls and two to the boys. Would next year's competition end in a draw or a clear lead for the Swotto girls?

The Round House

What goes on in this building? Well, it is the main meeting place for leaders or representatives from all four Quadrants. In front of the building each Quadrant has its own triangular area with attractive gardens, pathways and parking areas leading up to the reception lounge where you can look at documents and photos and listen to recordings, all on the TerraNet to find out everything you want to know about the history and modern life of each Quadrant. Through a door at the back of the reception lounge the delegates and journalists who take part in meetings, enter the large, beautifully furnished meeting room of the 'Terrament'. Apart from the preparation of material for the Jurassica

Journal, this is the room where important discussions, negotiations and decisions are made by those who sit at a large round table.

The four Quadrants all have different coloured seats so they can easily be seen from the Public Gallery and where each of the leaders is sitting. When meetings are in progress it is also possible to identify those taking part because each representative has to wear sweatshirts in the winter and t-shirts in the summer designed by each Quadrant. Each of these T-shirts or sweatshirts has a clear motif or logo printed on the back.

Those from Terrasnotta wear yellow shirts with a picture of a collection of tasty-looking Bogey cakes in shades of green. Those from Terrablotta wear light purple shirts with a picture of red bogberries and white snowberries. Those from Terraposha wear blue shirts with a picture of a bright red PMW and finally those from Terraswotta wear cream coloured shirts with a picture of an open book with the words TERRA written above the book and SWOTTA below the book, both in fancy dark brown writing.

Although most of the produce from each Quadrant is used, eaten or drunk by the inhabitants of that area, there is regular movement of goods from one Quadrant to another. For example, there are many Bogey bars outside Terrasnotta where people can tuck into bogey cakes washed down with a glass or two of bogberry or snowberry wine from Terrablotta.

Those who earn lots of money in the cities are often seen driving around in PMWs and each Quadrant, particularly in Terraposha, has a good selection of books and glossy magazines from Terraswotta. So generally business was good, prices were fair and everyone seemed fairly happy until the time that the 'white dot' in the Astrasky became real and threatening.

Astraflop

One day, the leaders of the Terrament had gathered round the table and started to talk about something very unusual which was visible in the night sky. What looked like a shiny blob had been spotted far, far away in the Astrasky millions of miles from Terra. Some people said that it sparkled and twinkled just like a star.

"What could it be?" everyone was asking.

Nobody knew! There were lots of discussions and suggestions in all four Quadrants on the television and on the radio. If not a star or a planet, perhaps it was an asteroid or a comet or even a space ship from another world?

From that moment, the nightly sight of this unknown object was very worrying indeed. As the weeks passed everyone could see that it was getting bigger and bigger and closer and closer to their world. Would it miss Terra and keep on hurtling through the Astrasky or would it hit them? The leaders of the Terrament now met on a daily basis in the Round House to discuss this threat to their lands. The public gallery was always full of people listening to the latest reports and looking at the up-to-the minute photographs of it taken from the mountain telescopes. The faces of the leaders gradually said it all. Yes, it was going to hit them. Emergency plans were hastily drawn up as to how the population of the four Quadrants must prepare themselves for the 'Big Bang.'

One winter's morning the whole population of the four Quadrants was woken up by a terrifying roar which was steadily getting louder and louder. Children frightened by this awful sound burst into tears, dogs barked, cats scuttled for cover and everyone rushed outside their homes to gaze in horror.

A huge white fiery ball with a long glistening tail just like a comet was approaching them at an incredible speed. Families dived for cover inside their homes, expecting their land to be blasted to pieces by this invader from the Astrasky, but much to their total surprise, it suddenly slowed right down and flopped onto the land with a big 'THUD', not a deafening bang followed by a Terra shattering explosion, just a big 'THUD' right on top of the Round House spreading its soft debris for about a thousand metres on each side of the Round House and into all four Quadrants. When settled, the height of this soft invader from the Astrasky reached about twenty metres above the roof of the Round House which, of course, was now completely buried.

There was much relief, tears, hugging and kissing everywhere. Nobody had been killed or even hurt, there didn't seem to be any structural damage to buildings and slowly from all corners of the Quadrants people came to gaze, both in wonder and fear, at this huge black dollop of Astradust. When touched, this fine dust, just like ash from a fire, slipped through the fingers and floated to the ground with absolutely no smell and leaving no marks on the skin. The citizens went on to name this astral phenomena 'The Astraflop.'

Happy, Snappy Times

For about two years after the arrival of this 'Astraflop' as it was called, thousands of people had gradually removed most of the dust from the fields and low hills around the Round House. It was discovered that the dust was truly amazing stuff.

In Terrablotta it had been liberally scattered over the bogberry swamps and over the snowberry slopes resulting in the best harvests of berries they had ever seen.

In Terrasnotta it was a similar story, the bogey grass harvests had produced the finest grass for bogey flour and the thickest stems for snot oil in the recorded history of the Quadrant.

In Terraswotta they found that by adding this black dust to wood pulp they could produce the most amazing quality paper for their books, journals, magazines and newspapers. When added to various processes for making photographs, the end result produced perfect glossy images the likes of which had never been seen before.

In Terraposha they realised that by adding the dust to the mixture in their car sprays, the paintwork on their PMWs shone so brightly and was so long-lasting, they just couldn't keep up with the demand for it. The car exteriors not only shone but the leather seats also looked extra shiny, once the dust was wiped off them. The Terraposha Equestrian School of Dignified Horsemanship was also delighted with the dust as their horses' saddles, bridles and stirrups gleamed like never before.

However, because of the huge demand for the remaining dust, this is when the cross border scuffles and fights began. Everyone wanted to collect the remaining Astradust, even if it meant stealing from their neighbours. In the middle of the night there were noisy spade and shovel fights as greedy dust robbers either on foot or in four track vehicles crossed over fields and onto the low border hills clutching their bags and sacks. These thieves filled them up as quickly as possible and then raced back across the border to the safety of their own Quadrant.

After several weeks of border scuffles and lots of anti-neighbour TV coverage, each Quadrant posted tough looking border patrols where the remaining pockets of the valuable dust could be found. Slowly but surely, this remaining treasure was limited to the large pile still covering the Round House roof. Most people believed that the dust robbers wouldn't dare to enter this forbidden area. Everyone wondered how this impressive heap of black dust could be fairly and evenly split between the four Quadrants. Well, they didn't have to ponder over this conundrum for very long!

During the very early hours of one winter morning, small groups of people wearing dark clothes took advantage of the cold, clear moonlit night to very quietly approach the Round House from each of the four private triangular Quadrant parks. By sheer coincidence, these four bands of dust robbers had chosen the same time to attempt to steal the remaining large pile of Astradust from the Round House roof. They were equipped with small bags, large bags, spades, shovels, long ladders and sticks. As soon as each little group had crossed their Quadrant gardens and car park; all of which had been cleared of Astradust some time ago; they silently placed their extended ladders against their section of the building and prepared to climb. As the first climbers reached the long rain gutter running all around the Round House, they were immediately aware that they were not alone. Faint torch lights could be seen to their right and to their left accompanied by a great deal of muttering and cursing from the gathered dust robbers.

"We've got company," hissed Snotto Sebastian. "There are others up here going after the dust as well."

"Let's go for it!" shouted his fellow robbers from Long Wetnose Farm who really wanted the remaining dust for their next bogey grass harvest.

Not far away to the right, Sebastian had been spotted by Barnaby the Blotto as he clambered onto the roof. Barnaby was there with the boys from South Blott Farm and needed the remaining dust for their marsh and mountain berries. Further to the right, Barnaby was spotted by Tarquin the Posho who was there with four of his friends from the 'PB'. Tarquin's dad owned the main car spray factory in Terraposha and desperately wanted the remaining dust so he could continue to sell the finest quality paint sprays in the Quadrant. Further around again, in the Terraswotta triangle, Tarquin spotted Dicky Lemon and Spud Doolittle. These ex-Swotto Fallouts, now living in Terrablotta, had come along and had climbed over into the Terraswotta triangle. They had climbed up a drain pipe onto the roof with the intention of taking as much dust as they could, to sell to a man whom they had met the day before. This man published books, newspapers and magazines and had told Dicky and Spud that he would pay 'a very, very good price' for any bags of remaining dust they could get their hands on.

Almost at once everyone on the roof scrambled towards the topmost point where the largest pile of Astradust still lay untouched. What a noise! Everyone was shouting and swearing. Snotto Sebastian tried to push Blotto Barnaby off the roof with his long stick. Posho Tarquin tried to do the same to Fallout Dicky but tough Dicky grabbed hold of the stick and pushed Tarquin back onto his Posho friend, Rupert, who in turn fell against their ladder and all four tumbled back over the edge of the roof and down onto the soft ground a few meters below. Sebastian and Barnaby were now locked in combat pushing and shoving each other whilst trying to retain their balance on the slippery, sloping surface of the roof.

All the others in the Snotto and Blotto gangs piled in on top of each other, whilst Dicky and Spud, now back on the roof saw their chance. With the other two gangs shouting and fighting they started to grab as much dust as they could. They stuffed it into one bag after another, throwing them down into the garden below. Within seconds their bags were spotted by the other two gangs who were still pushing, punching and shoving each other. The roof scrapping stopped immediately as Barnaby's boys and Sebastian's gang raced over to Dicky and Spud to try and grab the last precious bags of Astradust. Who got the dust? Well, at this crucial moment things were about to change.

The Big Suck Up

The remaining dust robbers on the Round House roof and most of the inhabitants of the planet Terra were suddenly aware of a new dreadful sound coming from the Astrasky. It started as a high pitched wail which became increasingly louder, making people cover their ears to block out the awful din. The noise changed to a throaty sound like the sucking of a giant vacuum cleaner. To the utter amazement of those near the Round House, the remaining heaps of dust on the roof and on the ground were being sucked back up into the sky in long straight white lines, higher and higher back into the Astrasky. The black dust seen for so long on the ground had turned white as its return to the the dark, cloudless night sky was very clearly seen by thousands of open mouthed onlookers.

Frightened out of their wits, the roof dust robbers dropped everything, climbed down their ladders and ran as fast as they could away from the Round House. After about fifteen minutes it was all gone, every last speck of it. Then the sucking sound suddenly stopped. A long eerie silence followed. Nobody spoke for what seemed like an eternity. Everyone was totally dumbfounded by the incredible scene they had just witnessed.

Gradually, little groups of Snottos, Blottos, Swottos and Poshos carefully made their way to the Round House expecting to see a scene of total ruin and devastation. Not so. The Round House looked as it always had, as did the gardens and the car parks around it. People peered through its big windows and were so surprised to see that there was no damage at all to the building, despite the enormous weight of the dust, which had settled on top of it for such a long time.

Once the area had been thoroughly checked by safety teams and security guards, the Quadrant leaders gathered in the Terrament meeting room for the first time in over two years to discuss what to do next. Everyone agreed that it was 'party time', a chance to join together and to celebrate the fact that no one had been killed or seriously injured and nothing had suffered damage from the falling and subsequent vacuuming of the Astradust.

The Poshos chose to celebrate around their swimming pools and in their large homes holding lavish parties for all their stylish friends. The Swottos also celebrated in their homes and held parties in the Gramma Halls attached to their large universities and colleges. The Snottos and the Blottos were mainly to be found celebrating in pubs, clubs, hotels and village halls consuming large quantities of bogey cakes and drinking bottle after bottle of excellent bogberry and snowberry wine.

After days of individual quadrant merry making, a big all-Quadrant celebration took place in the enormous Round House restaurant and theatre. The evening's entertainment was broadcast on all Quadrant television stations and on the TerraNet. A sumptuous meal and a great deal of singing and dancing continued well into the early hours.

However, before it got too late a ten year old Swotto girl was congratulated for writing a poem about the Astraflop as part of a Jurassica-wide primary school competition. The happy smiling girl left the stage amid great applause holding her specially framed copy and a t-shirt on which her poem had been printed. The poem went like this:-

'From the Astrasky it raced non stop
When it hit us, not a big BANG - an AstraFLOP.

We used its fine dust to improve our pages
I really hoped it would last for ages.
Its remains were sucked by a power from above
White beams of dust climbing higher and higher
Leaving memories and images right here on our Terra
Which I know will stay with me forever and ever.'

Much later on, in a nearby hotel, two Blottos were gazing skywards while enjoying a small glass of bogberry wine before bed time when Blotto Bill said to Blotto Ben,

"You see that white spot Ben right above us?"

"Yes," Ben replied, "I have noticed it."

"Well," said Bill, "I'm sure it's much bigger now than it was last week."

"No, you're imagining things," muttered Ben.

He turned to look at his friend.

"Anyway, once is enough my good friend. You don't honestly believe it could happen again, do you?"

They both stared at the bright, white spot.

"Do you hear that noise Ben?" said Bill.

"Yes… and I think I've heard it before!"

The Amazing Christmas Light Show

Kirsty was fed up. In just over two weeks it would be Christmas Day and yet somehow she didn't feel very Christmassy at all. Maybe this Christmas, usually favourite time of the year, would slip by unnoticed. As for her parents, uncles and aunts, in fact every adult she knew, all they seemed interested in was what was happening up there in the night sky.

It was their only topic of conversation and they hadn't stopped talking about it for days, or was it weeks? What was so important about those particular stars anyway? Like everyone else, Kirsty had noticed that over the past few weeks there seemed to be fewer and fewer stars twinkling above their house in the evening, but surely things couldn't be that bad, could they?

Every time the news came on the radio or television, people talked about a shift in the earth's orbit or something like that. What was it that funny man with the big nose had said yesterday, she thought. Oh yes, 'The end of the world is upon us'. Well, if it really was that bad, she considered crossly, they should all try to forget about it and have the best Christmas ever before everything blew up.

With great sadness running through her, Kirsty leaned towards her desk and placed her elbow on it, supporting her chin with her hand and gazed out at the night sky. In the distance she could see Golden Cap and the twinkly of lights of Charmouth, but high up above in half of the cloudless sky it was black, inky black, quite scary really, and the other half of the sky wasn't much better, just a few bright specks to be seen.

She recalled one hot summer night many months ago when she last sat at her desk looking out at the universe. What a difference. She'd seen millions of bright specks everywhere, but now it was almost total blackness. She thought about the man with the big nose again. Maybe he was right, maybe when these last few stars disappear, we might all vanish into thin air.

She sat up, switched on her desk light, took out a pencil, a sheet of writing paper and decided there and then to write a letter to Father Christmas. It was the 10th December so he should receive her letter in good time before he set off to deliver the presents. What she wanted most of all was the beautiful, big doll she'd gazed at longingly at in the toy shop window, to be mother or teacher to her large collection of little dolls.

Just before Kirsty signed her name at the bottom of the note she thought it might be a good idea to tell Father Christmas what had been spoiling Christmas so far this year. She decided to ask if he might be able to do something about it.

The letter was posted the following day and over the course of the next seven days things got a little better. Kirsty took part in the end of term school nativity play, then a few days later went with her Mum, Dad and elder brother Jack to the local church to sing carols. She also helped her Mum make mince pies and went shopping with her at the weekend.

On the 18th December at about 3 o'clock in the morning, Kirsty awoke from a very deep sleep. For a short while she felt afraid although she didn't really know why. She kept her eyes tightly shut and pulled the bed clothes up over her head. Slowly she emerged from underneath the covers. She opened her left eye, then the right. She felt sure it was the middle of the night but wondered why could she see all around her room. She sat up fully in her bed. No lights were on, no moon was shining and there was hardly a star left, yet there was a funny blue grey light everywhere. She couldn't make things out clearly but looking at the gap in the slightly open door she felt certain that there was a brighter light just outside her room. Perhaps somebody had gone downstairs to the kitchen or had forgotten to turn off the landing light.

Instead of settling back down under the sheets Kirsty sat puzzled, looking around. It was hard to explain yet she felt as if someone (or something) was calling her through the strange hazy light, pulling her towards an encounter she would never forget. There was no doubt about it, she would have to get up and investigate.

She wrapped her dressing gown tightly around her body and cautiously opened the bedroom door. The landing light was turned off and the hazy illumination seemed to get stronger towards the bottom of the stairs. The weird light drew her ever onwards, past Jack's room, past her parent's bedroom then slowly downstairs towards the living room. At the bottom of the stairs she peered down the long passageway towards the rest of the house. The kitchen appeared to be in total darkness but behind the half closed door of the living room, the light seemed to get stronger again.

Kirsty pushed opened the door cautiously and walked inside. Just like her bedroom, she was able to make out most of the familiar items in the room but as she turned towards the fireplace she froze. Her heart missed a beat and her mouth opened wide as she gulped an entire breath of air. Disbelieving eyes stared at the incredible sight which confronted her.

Sitting on a stool right by the fireplace was the kindly old gentleman to whom she had written a week earlier. Yes, right there in front of her, almost within touching distance, was Father Christmas dressed in red and white splendour and wearing white fur-trimmed boots. His round face radiated a welcoming smile towards the astonished nine year old girl. They looked at one another for almost a full minute before this most unexpected visitor broke the silence.

"Thanks for your letter Kirsty," said Father Christmas. "Yes, you're quite right, I'm also terribly worried about the disappearing stars, because I need them all to guide me on my sleigh on the 24th. Without them, I probably won't be able to deliver the mountain of presents I have all wrapped up and ready to go". He was silent for a moment, "However," he continued, "I do have a plan."

Kirsty sat on the arm of her father's fireside chair, quite close to Father Christmas. For about fifteen minutes she listened carefully to what he had to say. He talked about her town and the Christmas tree with its coloured lights and carols being sung around it by children of all nationalities just before Christmas. Finally, he held out his hand and gave Kirsty an object that resembled a long coiled tongue of rubbery plasticine. As she touched it, a sharp tingle rather like a small electric shock raced through her body. She placed it in the palm of her hand and gently squeezed it, smelled it, then carefully placed it in her dressing gown pocket.

When she looked up, Father Christmas had gone.

With his instructions fresh in her mind she went back upstairs to her room and within seconds of getting back into bed the blue grey light faded away into the darkness.

Later that day around the breakfast table she recounted her amazing tale to Jack and her parents. They listened politely then Jack (two years older than her) left the table saying her dream sounded like a load of old rubbish and that he was going out to see a friend.

Mum smiled and muttered, "Well, wasn't that a fantastic dream," then immediately busied herself clearing the breakfast table.

Dad said he thought having the children around the Christmas tree for a sing-song was a great idea and he'd mention it to his friend, the Mayor.

That night, over a drink at the Cobb Inn, the Mayor listened to his suggestion. She also thought a circle of children of around a Christmas tree was an excellent idea and agreed that the evening of 23rd December would be a perfect time to organise a few activities around the harbour. They planned to have a Father Christmas character housed in a painted wooden grotto distributing gifts to children, someone roasting chestnuts, another selling hot drinks. It would be a great opportunity to bring together the many families of different nationalities who lived in Lyme and the neighbouring towns and villages.

The mayor agreed to put advertisements in the local paper immediately, ring up the local radio stations and take care of all the other arrangements personally. Over the next few days Kirsty posted her Christmas cards and bought presents for her family, a few relations and one or two close friends.

After lunch on the 23rd, Kirsty and Jack went down to the harbour to watch the preparations for the evening's entertainment. All around them people were busily setting up their stalls, testing loudspeakers and decorating the brightly painted grotto and the cardboard reindeer and sleigh. Underneath the magnificent tree there were piles of empty boxes covered in Christmas wrapping paper. Jack wandered off to talk to his friends and Kirsty slowly circled the tree.

Whenever she saw a light bulb hidden amongst the pine needles she stopped, peeled off a small piece of the clear rubbery strip Father Christmas had given her and stuck it on the bulb. Fortunately for her there were quite a lot of bulbs towards the base of the tree so she managed to reach ten bulbs altogether quite easily. When she'd finished there was one last piece of the strip left and she tucked it away in the pocket of her coat.

As afternoon melted into evening only one twinkling star was left, marooned in a sea of blackness. Everyone, including some of her young friends, was asking the big question. What would happen to the world when that light went out? Kirsty couldn't help remembering what the man with the big nose had said on the telly.

The harbourside began to fill with people. Excited children queued up to visit Father Christmas in his grotto. A large smiling lady with a tall white chef's hat perched on her head was selling little bags of hot chestnuts. Coloured lights twinkled around the stalls that had been set up in the afternoon and were now selling novelty Christmas presents, hot drinks, bunches of holly, ivy and mistletoe, Christmas puddings and all sorts of other goodies.

From loudspeakers positioned here and there, Christmas carols could be heard everywhere and the Mayor and Town Councillors were delighted to see so many people coming into their town.

At 8.30pm precisely the Mayor cleared her throat, then over the loudspeakers she asked all the children to form a large circle around the Christmas tree to sing a carol together.

Kirsty noticed there were quite a number of families speaking in different languages and as the circle slowly formed around the tree, she felt certain it contained children from at least ten different countries.

With her heart pumping butterflies right through her body, Kirsty's warm, damp left hand took hold of the cool hand of her young neighbour and her right hand plunged deep into her coat pocket. She pressed the last strip of the rubbery substance into the palm of her hand and then gripped the soft, gloved hand of the girl on her right.

The youngsters listened to some instructions from the Mayor, then they all began to sing Away in a Manger. Half way through the carol, the children began to walk slowly around the tree and they continued singing their song.

The bright lights of the tree intermingled with dozens of bright white flashes from press photographer's cameras as they snapped the happy scene for the weekly papers.

Kirsty carefully scanned the ground in front of her as she walked and sang. She was looking for the electric cable for the Christmas tree. It was trailing along the floor near a small generator by one of the fishing boats which had been winched out of the water for repairs. The generator provided the power for hundreds of light bulbs that were draped all over the tree.

At last, she spotted it and it her heart fluttered with fear. She quickly let go of the gloved hand to her right, bent down, picked up the cable, squeezed the strip of rubbery tongue around it and whilst holding onto the cable, she grabbed her young neighbour's hand again. As she did so, Kirsty felt the same tingling sensation racing through her arm as she did when Father Christmas handed her the coil by the fireplace.

In a matter of seconds the coloured lights on the tree appeared to get brighter and brighter and brighter, then all the different colours seemed to dissolve into one blazing, bright white light. Surprised by the sudden fierce intensity of light, the singing stopped, hands were released and anxious parents pulled their children back to safety. The tree glowed so brightly now that everyone had to shield their eyes or look away. Gasps of amazement rose up from the crowd as the generator suddenly coughed and stopped, yet the tree continued to glow like a great beacon.

All the buildings around the harbour suddenly lit up. Daylight had returned to one corner of the town and Kirsty could see crowds of people standing beside the harbour in shop doorways or clustered behind windows. To look directly at the Christmas tree you would have needed seriously strong sunglasses.

Wailing sirens filled the night air as fire engines, ambulances and police cars raced to the scene. Above their noise, another great gasp emerged from the crowd as the intense white light suddenly changed colour to red, then to yellow, then green and on to blue, in fact to all the colours of the rainbow.

Yet another gasp came from the crowd as the rainbow of colours suddenly shot skyward, filling the blackness high above with piercing multicoloured beams of light. This was undoubtedly the most amazing laser light display anyone had ever seen and on and on it continued.

Down at the harbourside, some of the people had become quite concerned about what was going to happen next and they started to move away from the tree, but their space was soon occupied by others who desperately wanted to witness the spectacle in the sky.

A lone TV cameraman had his camera firmly fixed on what was going on and the newspaper reporters who were clutching their microphones were simply too enthralled to ask people questions about what had led up to this point.

Then all of a sudden, almost as quickly as it had started, the light show ended.

The coloured beams were no more and the white light snapped back into darkness. The generator coughed into life again and the little twinkling lights on the tree gave out their gentle brightness. The crowd began to surge forward towards the tree and they couldn't believe their eyes. Not one light bulb had exploded and not one scrap of the tree had been damaged. The boxes with pretend presents in were still hanging from the branches, all wrapped in Christmas paper, all entirely unmarked.

Kirsty's parents appeared seemingly from nowhere and her Dad muttered something about getting home as quickly as possible.

Some time later, dressed in her nightie and looking out of her bedroom window, Kirsty gazed down towards the harbour. She could just about make out the tree, a fire engine and a small group of people huddled around the remaining embers of the fire which was still busy roasting chestnuts.

Many hours later, as the daylight of Christmas Eve brightened her room, Kirsty was woken up by her mother.

"It looks like we're going to have a busy day love," her Mum said, as she sat on the edge of her bed. "There are some people downstairs from the local paper who'd like to have a little chat with you, about last night."

Kirsty smiled and nodded, then got up and dressed quickly and went down to meet the press.

Throughout the whole day, newspaper, radio and television people besieged their small home. Jack was sent dozens of times down to the corner shop to buy more tea, milk, sugar, biscuits, plastic cups and plastic plates. Kirsty's Mum had never made so many cups of tea in her life and all the mince pies she'd made in recent weeks were eaten by hungry reporters. In the front room, her Dad helped to set up and then eventually dismantle all sorts of technical recording equipment.

By the end of the afternoon the invasion was over and the armies of journalists had at last retreated beyond their front gate. All the family collapsed exhausted onto the settee, then chuckled and pointed as they watched themselves and saw their house on the national television news.

Just before they all sat down to eat their evening meal, there was yet another knock at the door.

"Oh, no!" said Kirsty's Dad, "Not another reporter. We've had enough for one day. I'll tell whoever it is to go away until after Christmas."

It was not a reporter, it was an excited neighbour who was hardly able to contain their excitement. He urged everyone to come outside into the garden quickly. Intrigued, they trooped out onto the front lawn.

"Look up!" shouted their neighbour. "Look up!"

They did and just like the Christmas tree the night before, they couldn't believe their eyes.

Instead of the usual near total blackness, the stars were beginning to reappear in the night sky. As every second passed more and more twinkling dots could be seen. It was almost as if someone was turning all the night lights back on again, illuminating the route for Father Christmas on his most important night of the year.

Everyone laughed with joy, then hugged and kissed one another with relief. The world wasn't going to end after all.

As the dawn light of Christmas Day crept into Kirsty's room, she woke up, rubbed her eyes then glanced at the objects that had been placed at the end of her bed. She spotted a large stocking stuffed with all sorts of small packages and beside it sat a large box wrapped in gold paper.

Filled with excitement Kirsty's trembling hands emptied the contents of the stocking onto her bed. She hardly dared to guess what might be in the beautiful gold box.

She unwrapped lots of little packages filled with pens, rubbers, hair clips, games, ribbons, things for her dolls house kitchen, chocolate, fruit and nuts, then she cleared away the wrapping paper and turned her attention to the big box.

The beautiful gold paper was carefully removed, then with fidgety fingers Kirsty opened the large white box that had been concealed inside it. She gazed at the contents and promptly burst into tears of absolute joy. Inside the box was the one thing she desperately wanted, it was the beautiful doll she'd seen in the toy shop window and completely fallen in love with.

She took it out, hugged it tightly then spotted a little envelope between the fingers of the doll's hands. It was beautifully written in red ink and simply said, 'To Kirsty with love from Father Christmas.' She opened the envelope, took out a small white card, turned towards her bedside lamp and read the following words:

The lights are back on,
It's Christmas Eve
And all world's Father Christmases
are ready to leave.
We'll all be back late
Tired, hungry and thirsty
But we'll have delivered all our presents
Thanks to our little friend Kirsty.

Magic Oxygen Publishing

breathing life into words

We hope you enjoyed the read!

For future literary purchases we'd like to encourage you to buy from your local independent bookshop.

They need your love, money and support and all of our titles are available to order there.

#ShopLocal #BeSustainable #MakeADifference #MOLP

About Magic Oxygen

Magic Oxygen Limited is a little green publishing house based in Lyme Regis, Dorset. It was founded in 2011 by Tracey and Simon West, who share an enormous passion for organic seasonal food, simple green living and advocating sustainable behaviours in local and global environments; they also share a common love of the written word.

They have published 20 titles from some outstanding authors over the last few years, including Bridport Prize winning Chris Hill and the much loved children's writer, Sue Hampton. They've also showcased exceptional talent from emerging authors; these include Connor Cadellin McKee, James Dunford Wood, Anthony Ravenwood, Izzy Robertson, Leslie Tate and more. They have several multi-disciplined authors who are also playwrights and graphic novel producers; these include Max Brandt, Mark James and Robert Windsor.

New titles are hitting the bookshelf this year from Heather Godfrey and Tony Lambert amongst others and if that weren't enough diversity, they also have self-help and environmental titles from Lilly Laine, Elizabeth J Walker and Tracey herself.

For the full range see MagicOxygen.co.uk/shop and remember, every title can be ordered from local or national bookshops, and online too (they favour small independent retailers which helps keep money in local communities). Magic Oxygen are also happy to fulfil orders - they might even have a signed edition to hand!

The Greenest Writing Competitions in the World

Magic Oxygen have founded a series of writing contests designed to uncover literary talent from writers around the world. The main one is the Magic Oxygen Literary Prize, fondly known as MOLP, which carries a prize fund of £3,000.

In 2016 they launched the Mini-MOLPs, 5 diverse writing contests with thought provoking themes inspired by international eco-awareness events. The winners will bag 10 fabulous paperbacks from the Magic Oxygen best sellers list, plus an additional unique special prize.

These contests have a powerful environmental impact, because every single submission to MOLP and the Mini-MOLPs results in a tree being planted in Magic Oxygen's tropical Word Forest in Bore, Kenya. All entrants are sent the GPS coordinates of their trees.

This pioneering international project is carefully coordinated by forestry expert, Ru Hartwell of Community Carbon Link. He chose Kenya for the Word Forest because trees planted near the equator are the most efficient at capturing carbon from the atmosphere and keeping the planet cool. Ru specifically chose Bore because it's a remote community that has suffered greatly from deforestation. The new saplings will eventually reintroduce biodiversity, provide food, medicine and water purifiers and will create an income for the village too.

For further details and to submit entries, visit MagicOxygen.co.uk then help our reforestation project by spreading the news on social media.

Mini-MOLP April 2016: Letter to the Planet - 350 words

Have fun deciding who your letter is from.
What have they got to say for themselves?
Take inspiration from ***Earth Day*** *or* ***National Gardening Week***

Mini-MOLP May 2016: Eco-Flash Fiction - 250 words

Conjure up pocket-sized literary magnificence
with an uplifting green slant.
Take inspiration from ***World Biodiversity Day***
or ***International Dawn Chorus Day***

Mini-MOLP June 2016: Sonnet for the Solstice - 14 lines

Wax lyrical with a Shakespearian style sonnet and
imagine it performed at the break of day on the solstice.
Take inspiration from ***World Environment Day*** *or* ***World Oceans Day***

Mini-MOLP July 2016: Postcard from the Park - 200 words

Pen a postcard-sized piece to anyone or anything,
with your arboreal thoughts and stories.
Take inspiration from ***National Parks Week*** *or* ***National Tree Day***

Mini-MOLP August 2016: Last Words Monologue - 400 words

The film is about to end, the last of a species is about to die.
Write the script of their parting words.
Take inspiration from ***World Honey Bee Day*** *or* ***World Elephant Day***

Lightning Source UK Ltd.
Milton Keynes UK
UKOW06f2342180416

272499UK00001B/5/P

9 781910 094013